I0818983

By Elizabeth Berg

Life: A Love Story

Earth's the Right Place for Love

I'll Be Seeing You

The Confession Club

Happy to be Here

Night of Miracles

The Story of Arthur Truluv

Still Happy

Make Someone Happy

The Dream Lover

Tapestry of Fortunes

Once Upon a Time, There Was You

The Last Time I Saw You

Home Safe

The Day I Ate Whatever I Wanted (stories)

Dream When You're Feeling Blue

The Handmaid and the Carpenter

We Are All Welcome Here

The Year of Pleasures

The Art of Mending

Say When

True to Form

Ordinary Life: Stories

Never Change

Open House

Escaping into the Open: The Art of Writing True

Until the Real Thing Comes Along

What We Keep

Joy School

The Pull of the Moon

Range of Motion

Talk Before Sleep

Durable Goods

Family Traditions

LIFE: A Love Story

LIFE:
A Love Story

A NOVEL

Elizabeth Berg

RANDOM HOUSE
NEW YORK

Random House
An imprint and division of Penguin Random House LLC
1745 Broadway, New York, NY 10019
randomhousebooks.com
penguinrandomhouse.com

Hardcover ISBN 978-0-593-44682-9
Ebook ISBN 978-0-593-44684-3

Printed in the United States of America

1st Printing

First Edition

Book Team: Production editor: Jennifer Rodriguez • Managing editor: Rebecca Berlant • Production manager: Sandra Sjursen • Copy editor: Beth Pearson • Proofreaders: Andrea Gordon, Deb Bader, Lisa Grimenstein

Book design by Susan Turner

The authorized representative in the EU for product safety and compliance is Penguin Random House Ireland, Morrison Chambers, 32 Nassau Street, Dublin D02 YH68, Ireland. https://eu-contact.penguin.ie

For my grandchildren:
Matthew, Katelyn, and Daniel Krintzman,
and Nathaniel Berta

Now's a good time, before the night comes on,
To praise the loyalty of the vase of flowers
Gracing the parlor table, and the bowl of oranges,
And the book with freckled pages resting on the tablecloth.

—from "Still Life" by CARL DENNIS

LIFE: A Love Story

Dear Ruth Eimers,

My name is Teresa McNair, and I am Florence Greene's neighbor and friend. I am writing with the sad news that Florence passed away two days ago, on the morning of July 1st. I found her sitting at her kitchen table dressed in a tweed suit, nylon stockings, and heels, and she had applied a fair amount of rouge to her cheeks. She also had a hat and gloves on the table next to her purse. The paramedic in the ambulance said it looked like she was intending to go somewhere.

I met Flo not long ago when she helped me to capture my runaway cat, and we quickly developed a deep friendship. I found her to be charmingly straightforward, cheerful, and full of what I can only call simple grace. I say "simple" not meaning grace without depth, but rather to differentiate it from a way of being that is perhaps a little elevated or self-aware. The grace I witnessed in Flo seemed not something she aspired to, but rather a natural part of her. Difficult as the world sometimes becomes for most of us, Flo seemed to hold an unalterable love and appreciation for it. She did not deny life's sorrows, but she chose to focus more on its compensations. There was as well a guilelessness about her, and a giving quality that did not leave much room for self-absorption.

As you may know, Flo had been diagnosed with a cancer for which there was no cure, so in that sense she certainly was dressed up "intending to go somewhere." Her attitude about the end of her life was philosophical; I believe she *wondered* about it more than she feared or grieved it. (Though she did once mention that she would miss apple pie made by someone who didn't skimp on cinnamon, and the sound of children at play, especially when they thought no adults were listening.)

Flo told me she had willed her house and its contents to you—you'll be hearing from her lawyer in a separate communication—and that she was writing the enclosed letter to let you know more about some of the things here. She said she also wanted to share some things about her life she felt were important to tell you, and asked that if she had not mailed this letter to you at the time of her demise, would I do so.

The letter is quite long, as you see, and I did not feel it was my place to read it. If, after reading it yourself, you have questions, I will try to answer them.

I'm not sure if Florence mentions this in her letter, but I am a death doula. In my work, I try to offer a grounding and consistent presence to people in uncertain times, and to assist them with the transition from life to death in as peaceful and mindful a way as possible. Sometimes people want help with clarification of medical terms, or someone to serve as intermediary in conversations with doctors or family members. Sometimes I am asked simply to sit close by clients in silence, in order to bear witness. I do not and cannot take away all suffering, but I hope to lessen it, and I try to teach clients to be open to new possibilities and perspectives, even or especially at the end of their lives—to understand how much living can be packed into a short amount of time, and to see that it is never too late for some very important realizations. In my time with Flo, though, I was the student, and it is not an overstatement to say that what I learned from her changed my life.

I will leave you now to Flo's letter. I too have written more than I intended to. But then, that was Flo: showing you the value of taking some time. The poet Dorianne Laux said, "Any good poem is asking you simply to slow down." In that respect, Flo was a poem.

This comes with heartfelt condolences, and with the hope that whatever words Flo has sent you will soften the blow of her leave-taking. I believe it would please her to think that was so.

Sincerely,

Teresa McNair

Two months earlier

Florence Greene sits up slowly, steadies herself at the edge of the bed, and regards the bright line of sunlight coming from beneath the shade. Another day. The wealth of it!

She walks over to the window and raises the shade to look out at her small and tidy front lawn, at her white fence lined with watercolor pansies. Aren't they ever something, she thinks. A paintbox in petals. Here comes a young woman jogging down the street wearing shorts and a sleeveless t-shirt and a baseball cap, her ponytail coming out of a hole in the back of the cap and swinging like a metronome. She has those white plugs in her ears that Flo thinks makes people look like aliens. Three houses away, coming down the front steps, is a woman whom Flo has seen but not properly met; Flo doesn't even know her name. She looks like she's about fifty, and the expression on her face is always earnest and a little bit sad, rather like that of a child who's been chastised and has vowed to do better. She's walking quickly toward her car, parked on the street, carrying a large duffel bag over her shoulder. Flo has heard of people who go to private homes to do hair; maybe she's one of those. It used to be that Flo knew all her neighbors, but the block has turned over, and most people keep to themselves. At night, if you look in their windows, mostly what you see are TV screens so big they remind Flo of drive-in movies.

Well, she must get to it. She dresses in a blue shift and sneakers, washes up in the hall bathroom, and makes her way downstairs and into the kitchen, where she measures out coffee for four cups. While it brews, she sits at the little round table where last night she put out a never-before-opened box of floral stationery and a blue ballpoint pen. After she has her raisin toast and coffee, she'll begin. She wants to write to Ruthie, the woman who as a child grew up next door, and with whom Flo has kept in touch since Ruthie married and moved away. They don't write often, but they write honestly; even when Ruthie was a little girl she had never cottoned much to small talk. When she was twelve years old, Ruthie had asked Flo, "Do we bare our souls to each other?" and Flo had answered, "I believe we do."

"Fine, then," Ruthie had said. "Because later on I have some important things to tell you." She'd held up a finger in the air. "Important with a *capital I*."

Now Flo thinks she has some Important things to tell Ruthie. Where to start is the thing. Flo has a sudden image of herself backing into the kitchen one hot summer day many years ago, her arms laden with tomatoes and flowers from the garden. Here she came, pushing through the screen door with her hind end, her husband, Terrence, sitting at the table with his newspaper and coffee, watching her. "Why don't you try coming in *front*wards?" he had asked, and she'd said, "This is just how I do."

So then.

Dear Ruthie,

I only wish I'd have gotten a chicken to keep in the backyard, that's what I'm thinking right now. I always did like chickens, from the time I was a little girl and first held a chick in my hand, light as air and peeping away, and I could hardly move from sheer delight, those little orange feet sticking out of a ball of fluff, you'd never think there was flesh and bones in there, seemed like those chicks were something you could wish on and blow away. But talking about chickens, for heaven's sake, at a time like this! What I mean is, I have gotten a bad prognosis for a cancer that has reared up and taken off, and my doctor told me that I might want to put my affairs in order. When he told me, a blush crept into his face—bless his heart, he felt bad. I'm ninety-two, I told him, and patted his hand. Still, he said, and I had to agree with him there.

I hope this won't make you too sad, Honey. I know you too are dealing with some bad news, I read *your* last letter about your planning to divorce. I have some things to say about that, too, but later.

I have about a month, maybe six weeks. Did you ever think that a little interval of time like two weeks could mean so much? But here comes the voice in my brain begging for those fourteen extra days I might be given. Begging! Even an old woman like me who can't see good or walk far and whose very blood is humming with the going-home song, why I'm still ginned up for more time. I'll tell you true, I would live a hundred lifetimes back-to-back if I could, but I can't.

Oh, I always did hate that word "can't." I didn't *believe* it. People would tell me you can't do this, and you can't do that, and it was like I had a barrier in my brain where in the front part I listened politely but behind the barrier I was thinking the hell you say. But I got to face facts now, and so here's what, Ruthie.

I want to leave my house and everything in it to you. Perhaps you might be wanting to come back here now to live? I remember last year when you came home for a visit, you left your children with your parents in that condo they moved to and you and I walked around the block slow and you told me things you loved about this neighborhood, and you shared many memories you had of it. We stopped by the Filmores' towering oak tree, I remember, and you got teary and put your hand on my arm and said, Oh, Flo, but then you never finished. I spect the trouble had started in your house around then. I remember I said to you, You know you can tell me anything, and you said you weren't sure what to say or how to say it, you hardly knew yourself all you were feeling. You said, I'll tell you once I've decided what I'm doing, and I said that's fine and didn't either one of us say another word about it but I could see the weight in you, Ruthie, it never did lift the whole time you were home. And I hurt for you as I always did when you were suffering, whether it was your crying your eyes out over a toy you lost or the time when your first boyfriend broke up with you right after your thirteenth birthday. (That's *it* for boys! you told me. I will ***never*** love ***again***! I said gentle, You may not think so now, but things change. NO THEY DON'T you said, you were in that terrible phase of yelling when you were upset. You said, I am just going to be a VETERINARIAN! And I said, Could you speak up? I didn't hear that. And then you had to smile and so did I.)

Anyway, I hired a lawyer to prepare the necessary papers for leaving everything to you, and they are signed and ready to go. He will send them on to you when the time comes. Meantime, I would like to tell you some things I never told you before, especially something that I've wanted to tell you for years. Do you remember the day you asked me what had I been doing out there in the backyard behind the roses? My heart ricocheted in my chest. I had no idea anyone had seen me, and I was scared to death you were going to investigate for yourself and discover my secret, you were always a most determined child, so I told you I was burying ground-up dead things to fertilize the plants, I figured that would keep you away and it sure enough did. But that is not what I was doing, and I'm going to work up to telling you the truth about what I was burying.

I also want to tell you about some of my favorite things in my house, many of which bring back memories that I cherish. Lately, though, it seems there's more to those things than that. I look in a drawer or a cupboard and I think, Oh, I got to tell Ruthie about this. You can do with my things whatever you like but I just think you should know why they are not just objects, but pieces of my life that point to something ***bigger*** than my life. I'll tell you what, a rubber band is not just a rubber band, as you will come to see.

I might have cared about my things too much. Terrence and the Good Lord used to warn me about that, each in his own way, but I couldn't help loving some things the way I did. Take my dishes with the little pink roses on them. One time I kissed a saucer after I dried it off and wasn't that the exact time that Terrence came into the kitchen and stopped and said, What are you doing? and I said, Nothing, and we just let that one go, which if you ask me is 99% of a good marriage, knowing when to let something go. I also very much loved a silver frame with a picture of my daddy out in the fields, his foot on a tractor and his black hair hanging a little in his eyes, his arms crossed all muscley. I thought my daddy could just about move mountains, and to me that picture proved it.

I wanted to write all this out rather than tell you, Ruthie. I believe that something happens in the writing out of things, and in the reading of them, that does not happen otherwise. I think you believe that, too, and that's why I have so many letters from you and I have kept every one in my bottom dresser drawer. My favorites are the ones where you talked about having your babies. I felt I was right in the delivery room with you, the drama was better than those cop shows. And I liked when you told me about your children's antics, there is so much of what I remember about you in them. You sent one letter when you were up early on Christmas Day, getting the turkey ready, and you sat at your kitchen table and wrote me out the whole menu and you said you wished I could be there and so did I. You seemed so happy. Snow was falling and you told me how pretty it looked and said you would never forget the snowball fight you and I had against Terrence and your brother and WE WON.

Writing to you always makes me feel like I'm visiting with you. Course, it is just me talking here, but I see your face while I'm writing out these words, and sometimes I imagine pretty good what you might say back.

But about the house and all the things in it. I hope this letter will give you a record in case you forget what something is and why it mattered, and also I suppose it is a legal document. I guess I could have it notarized, I have a friend who is a notary public and you would think that makes her president of the U.S. of A., but let us allow our friends what they need so long as it doesn't harm anyone else, why not. I'll tell you what, though, that notary public, Jeannie Drummond is her name, she makes the best boysenberry pie you ever did taste. I wonder why we don't all have t-shirts made up with some of our good things on them. Imagine, you get on the bus and sit next to someone whose t-shirt says: ***Champion bowler! I speak Chinese! Trained my dog to pray!*** It could ease some of the world's tensions, I think. A lot of things could ease the world's tensions that we don't bother with, I never have understood why. I never have understood why we go from one war to the next to the next to the next. All those young men, cut off from all they could have done. And young women, too. After World War II started, I used to ask Terrence why there had to be war, why? and he would always sigh and say, Flo, it's always been that way since time immemorial, and I would say but why? and he would say it's human nature, and I would say, I don't believe that, I believe goodness is human nature, and he would hold up his coffee mug asking for a refill like I was his own personal waitress which I guess I was though I didn't mind a bit since he was my personal garbage man and mechanic and confronter of things in the night. But that was the end of that conversation. Human nature. Since time immemorial. Then Terrence got called up for service, and we didn't either one of us talk any more about why there had to be war. We just prayed for his safe return. Every night he was in France, I knelt at the side of my bed and prayed with all my might for him to come back to me safe and sound, and I vowed that if he did, there would be nothing, *nothing* that would ever make us part. Right after he returned, I tried to ask him what it had been like over there, but he didn't want to talk about it. It was not for the reason I thought. Naturally, he was troubled by the great loss of lives, by the horrifically wounded, but something else happened over there and it took many years before we talked about it.

I have so much to tell you, but don't feel you have to read this all at once. Tell you what, I'll take my time writing it, you take your time reading it.

Flo puts down the pen and massages her hand. She could write more, she really could! But here is the doorbell and she goes to see who's there. It's Denise, her next-door neighbor.

"I hate to bother you," Denise says, and Flo opens the door wider and gestures for her to come in. But Denise says, "Oh, I'd love to, but I'm in the middle of a recipe and I'm out of one of the ingredients."

"Would I have it?" Flo asks.

"Sumac?" Denise asks.

"Say what?"

"Sumac. It's a Middle Eastern spice. Kind of tangy."

"What are you making?"

"Oh, just some chicken dish. That's all I ever make is chicken anymore. I'm *tired* of cooking."

"Me, too," Flo says.

"Well, you're entitled," Denise says, and Flo knows Denise means by virtue of Flo's age. She considers telling Denise The News, but elects not to.

"Can you watch Champ while I run over to the grocery store?"

"Course I can."

"I'll go and get him," Denise says. "*Thank* you."

Flo knows Denise's dog doesn't like to be left alone anymore and she's glad she can babysit him. He has been a friend of hers since the day he came home as a six-week-old befuddled little speck of white. They've gotten old together; it wouldn't surprise Flo if they could share some of their medications. Sometimes of an evening they're both sitting on their front porches and Champ will look over at Flo and she thinks he's saying a mouthful in a gaze. Oftentimes, the dog will amble on over and sit by her and they'll have a conversation, each commenting in their own way about what they see. Champ might see a squirrel run up a tree and tense up, but he just doesn't have it in him to run after anything anymore. But "That's the way, Champ," Flo will tell him. "You watch him!" She likes to think that preserves his dignity. Sometimes Champ seems to think he sees things that are nothing at all, and Flo tells him the same thing, "That's right, you watch, now!" And he does, his gaze steady, his bearing as proud as a marble lion. Flo likes to give Champ potato chips, just a couple. It makes her laugh to hear him crunch them exactly like a person.

Here comes Champ now, held in Denise's arms and carefully deposited in Flo's front hall. "I'll be back soon," Denise says.

"Don't rush," Flo says.

She closes the door after Denise and looks down at Champ staring up at her with his cloudy eyes. She pats her leg for him to follow her into the living room, but he stands firm. "You want to go on the porch?" she asks him, and there goes his tail moving back and forth like a windshield wiper.

"Okay," she says. "Let me get my sweater."

Outside, Champ thumps down at his place near the top step, one of his paws crossed over the other as elegant as Alistair Cooke on *Masterpiece Theatre*. Flo sits in the rocker and moves back and forth. Nothing like a rocker, really.

"Champ!" Flo says.

He turns toward her.

"Would you like to come up here and rock with me?"

Champ cocks his head like she's asked if he wants a cookie, but makes no move to get up.

She pats her lap. "Come on up, it's nice."

Now he looks away. Not interested. Well, you can't expect someone to like something just because you do. Especially if you're a dog who sees another dog walking down the sidewalk who apparently needs a good dressing down.

Champ rises up on stiff legs and goes to the edge of the porch step. He barks—one, two, three times—and then watches through squinty eyes as the dog and the owner keep walking.

"Good job, Champ," Flo says. "I agree that dog was up to no good. I always did say you can't trust a wiener dog. They rely too much on their cuteness, and next thing you know they've dug up all your dahlia bulbs."

Champ puts his muzzle on his paws, closes his eyes. Denise told her the other day that mostly what Champ was now was a rug, but she said it with deep affection.

"Are you bored, Champ? Do you want to go for a walk?"

No response. What would he say, if he could talk? She can just imagine it: *Nah, thanks, Flo, but a walk just isn't the same anymore. Maybe you feel the same way.*

Flo says, "I kind of feel the same way, but you know, even if you go slow, you can still have a good time. Maybe even a better time than when you hurry along. You see more."

True, she imagines him saying. *And there's nothing like those smells you encounter. Why is it that you people never give us enough time for smelling?*

"Oh, come on, Champ," Flo says. "Sometimes when I used to walk you, you would sniff at something seemed like for twenty minutes straight. I'd hold the leash all patient for a while, but then we really did have to move on."

You humans don't understand because your sense of smell is so poor. You're missing a whole universe of things.

"I spect you may have a point. We certainly like smelling flowers."

They're all right. But I've rolled in some things that—

"I know. You don't have to go into details."

And after we go to all the trouble to perfume ourselves, you humans wipe it off.

Flo looks up into the sky. "Isn't it a lovely day, though? Look at that sky."

No response from Champ, not even an imaginary one. He's sound asleep. Not a bad idea, a little nap with the warm sun on her face and the breeze so gentle. Something Flo has learned later in life is the value of a nap, how you awaken fresh and all start-overish.

Flo starts to close her eyes but then she hears a car horn beep and there is Denise coming up the driveway. She climbs Flo's porch steps and lifts Champ up into her arms.

"Hold on," Flo tells her, and she goes over to lift one of Champ's ears to whisper into it, "I love you."

Thank you, Flo. I feel good. I think I want a marrow bone.

To Denise, Flo says, "I think he just told me he wants a marrow bone."

"He *always* wants a marrow bone."

"Well, I was right, then."

"Thanks for watching him, Flo."

Back in her house, Flo makes a cup of ginger tea. She'll drink it, then go back out on the porch and maybe take that nap after all.

But here comes the sound of someone coming up her front porch steps again. Denise must have forgotten to tell her something. But when Flo opens the door, she sees another woman standing there, that serious-faced woman she's noticed who lives down the block.

"Sorry to disturb you," the woman says. "I'm Teresa McNair, your neighbor, and my cat is under your porch, and he won't come out."

"Well, let's us corral him," Flo says. "I'll take one side, you take the other."

It doesn't work. The cat slips past both of them and climbs the tree on the boulevard. Teresa says, "I can't lose him. I just *got* him! I haven't even named him!"

"You're not going to lose him," Flo says. "I'll get some food, maybe we can tempt him down with that. Keep an eye on him; I'll be right back."

Flo goes back into the house filled with an invigorating excitement; there is nothing she likes more than helping people. She opens a little can of salmon, dumps it onto waxed paper, and takes it back outside. "Come over here by the bushes and hide," Flo tells the woman. "I'll make a trail of salmon that leads right to you."

Teresa walks slowly over to the bushes in front of Flo's house and Flo can tell she doesn't believe this will work. Well, they'll see.

Flo goes to the base of the tree and calls up, "Here, kitty,

kitty, kitty." She sees the flick of a white tail, some green eyes peering down.

"Come and get it!" Flo says, making the trail, and then she walks back up onto her porch with extreme nonchalance. *Eat it or not, I don't care* is what she wants to convey. She thinks that if there's one thing cats don't like, it's for them to be told what to do. Sure enough, after a few seconds here comes the cat cautiously scaling down the tree. When it reaches the ground it begins eating. Flo bets Teresa wants to run after it, but she holds her position. When the cat is directly before her, eating the last offering, she grabs him.

"Thank you!" Teresa cries. "I live just three doors down. I've got to go to work, but after that, may I come back and thank you properly? Say, six o'clock?"

"Why, sure," Flo says, and goes back inside. Maybe she should put a little color on her face if she's going to be doing all this socializing.

In her makeup drawer, she finds an unopened sample tube of Pecan Peach lipstick. It's ancient, from when Avon used to come calling, and wasn't that always a pleasant break in the day, the Avon lady sitting beside Flo on the sofa in her nice dress and spreading out all her wares on the coffee table in such a way that you wanted everything?

Flo tries the lipstick and finds it still works well enough. There's all kinds of old makeup in the drawer; Flo was never very good about throwing things away. She digs through the drawer for a while, remembering how she used to get ready to go out with Terrence and when she came downstairs with her makeup on he would say, "Well, don't you look nice?" And Flo always thought he'd had no idea what she'd done *to* look nice, patiently putting on the mascara and the rouge and the lipstick. He didn't care. He just liked that she looked nice. But here was the thing about Terrence. She could be absent of any makeup at all, and he would still tell her she was beautiful. That was mostly in her younger years, but even when she got old he would tell her she was beautiful, and that warmed her far more than the compliments he gave her when she was young. Everybody's beautiful when they're young, even if they don't know it. And isn't it funny, it seems to Flo, that mostly they *don't* know it. Mostly they complain about their faults that no one else even sees.

Ruthie, I just found some old mascara in my top right dresser drawer. It's the old-fashioned kind in a case with a mirror and you wet the cake of mascara with the tiny little brush that comes with it. All one summer, you used to play with it, you in those big shorts you liked to wear because they were your sister's, your mouth often stained with purple popsicle. You liked for me to put that mascara on you and then I would make you a tinfoil crown and matching wand and one time you changed my philodendron into a handsome prince. That's what you said, and I had to clasp my hands under my chin and say, Ohhhh yes now I see. I wonder do you remember that.

In the drawer below the makeup is a jewelry box, and the best thing in there is my pearls. I don't care what you wear pearls with, they make everything look good. Terrence gave me those pearls one Christmas and I looked up at him, and at first, I couldn't even speak. But then I said, Terrence, I am going to wear these tonight and then we're taking them back, there is no way we can afford them. And he said, I know we can't. And that's why I got them for you. If we were rich, what pleasure would there be in my giving you such a thing? You wear them, they're to help you remember what you're worth.

Oh, he could be romantic, Terrence. But every now and then I would have to hope the neighbors couldn't hear us fussing. Not that they didn't have their own squabbles. I once had a neighbor ask me in the driveway, Did you hear me yelling at my husband last night? No, I said, what were you fighting about? Well, she said, let's go to your kitchen and have some coffee. I remember I got out my flowered cups and before she commenced to complaining she said how pretty those cups were and that she liked drinking out of them, they made the coffee taste better. Dorothy Potter, with her two big dimples and her naturally curly hair, she was a real pretty gal. I have an address book and if you look in there under P you'll find her. You'll see a star by her name, which means she died, I never had the heart to cross anybody out. You'll see her old phone number: ME 1-6995. ME for Melrose. I think those old telephone prefixes were nice, I was sorry to see them go. PL, Parkland. TW, Twinbrook. And of course who could forget BUtterfield 8. Elizabeth Taylor. I wonder if every time she looked in the mirror, she couldn't help but say yes indeed. But of course even she got old and then she was always fighting with fat. She got married an awful lot of times, I don't see how she could say her vows seriously after a certain point. I say, Think hard before the first one, and then stick to it. Otherwise, you're just going to trade one set of problems for another.

Dorothy Potter told me why she had been mad at her husband, and at the end of the telling she said she realized she hadn't needed to get that mad at him. I said I sure did understand that, and I told about how one time I was spitting mad at Terrence, and I'm here to tell you that spitting mad is a real thing, I was shouting hearty and real spit was flying out my mouth. This was in the early years before I figured some things out and I was taking everything he did personally, from leaving the john lid up to saying something I found insensitive. Well, I decided he didn't love me anymore. And I nearly had smoke coming out my ears, I was just raging, thinking of how he had said, I'll always love you, I'll always be kind, I'll always take care of you, he'd said it pretty as a preacher. And so I told him, I said, Never say always to me! He said, What??? I told him again, Never say always to me! And he said why not. And I said because there IS no always, that's why! There is only sometimes, and if a girl believes in always, her heart will be flat broken. As I can surely attest.

Terrence nodded. He was so calm it made me kind of suspicious. But then he said, Sometimes there is always. When it comes to my loving you, for instance. I can't help it if you don't always feel it. But it is always there. It is there as long as I breathe in and out, and if I have my way it will be there long after I stop breathing and my bones have gone to dust.

I said, Don't you say those things to me when I'm so mad. And he said don't you tell me what to do! And then he said like this: Whooeee, I don't like a woman telling me what to do! And then we both busted out laughing and he said, Let me ask you something. Wouldn't you rather go out and eat than fight this way? And we went out for hamburgers to our favorite place and everything was better.

They sold trinkets at that restaurant we went to. One of them was a plastic toothpick dispenser with some little red flowers painted on it. You can't hardly make out the flowers anymore, but they were there. I said how I would like that dispenser and Terrence said he thought it was unnecessary, if you wanted a toothpick why you just pulled one out of the box. I went quiet then. We left and started walking home and I was awful quiet. And then Terrence pointed to a park bench we were passing and he told me to wait there and didn't he go back to the cafe and get me that toothpick dispenser. And he got down on one knee to give it to me like it was a diamond ring. But of course he didn't propose, he only said, Here you go, I'm sorry I didn't get it right away, and I said thank you, and when we got home I set up that toothpick dispenser and he tried it out and he said okay I see what you mean, even though I'm not sure he did. Whenever I come across that toothpick dispenser, I think about that time when he tried so hard. If you ever have seen something like a guy with real big, rough hands giving something dainty to a woman, that's how it was. Him thinking, I don't for the life of me know why we need something like this, but I guess she wants it.

When we finished walking home that night, I remember Terrence was talking about how great it must be to be a movie star. I told him I would never want to be a movie star. Really? he said, and I said really, I would not, I always think movie stars are mostly pining away in their big houses, always unsure and lonely, and who are they going to admit that to?

I said, Don't you think it would be a hard thing, having to pretend you live the high life all the time? I guess it would, Terrence said. Tell you what, I said. I have what I want. I want to be able to walk home in the dark with you, holding hands. I pointed to a streetlight and said, See? Our own spotlight.

And then Terrence said, Come with me, and he pulled me over to be under a tree and he kissed me so tender and said, I will never be able to tell you how much you mean to me. So you see, Ruthie, every time I see that toothpick dispenser, I remember that. That's why I kept it. I spect you'll throw it out now, and I guess you should. But anyhow you got the story, which is the important part.

You know, when Terrence got down on one knee to give me the toothpick dispenser, I remembered how I always thought that that was how he'd propose to me. But that's not the way he did it. I guess he was too shy. He proposed to me on the phone, my mother in the background banging on the piano so loud I could hardly hear him. What did you say? I asked. And he said again, I'm asking you to marry me, Flo. My heart like to rose up clean out of me. I said, Why are you asking me on the phone? He said well if I refused him he wouldn't have far to run to his bedroom and cry. I said ha ha. And then I said, But what about the ring part? I was just dying for an engagement ring I could look at a hundred times a day. He said, If you'll say yes, I'll sure enough bring it right over. I said yes and he brought over the ring and we went out in my backyard and he gave it to me right by the clothes pole. It's just a speck of a diamond, but I'll tell you what, it took my breath away and it still does. My engagement ring that Terrence gave me. I don't know that anyone would ever really appreciate it, worn thin on the band and so fragile now. I thought about being buried with it but that seemed selfish, seemed like it should live on somehow. It's not worth much, leastwise not in money. But maybe you could give it to some little girl might be thrilled to death with it, a real diamond ring. Tell her it was from a princess found her prince. I guess it's not correct anymore to say that, but I sure don't see why not. If you say a princess found her prince, doesn't it just mean a prince found his princess, too, and what's wrong with that? It's just two people both found a four-leaf clover is how I see it. And you know full well a person can find a four-leaf clover since didn't you come banging up onto my porch one summer day lit up like a

Christmas tree on account of you had found one. What should I do with it? you asked and I said well you just keep it. What if it dies and gets all shriveled up and blows away? you asked. I said then you just keep the memory that you found it. That's not going to blow away anywhere.

Now, Terrence was right romantic and we were happy together. But there was that secret I kept that I mentioned earlier and I believe I should finally tell you about it. It will take a bit of time for me to explain, and it will be hard for me to explain, so I want to wait a bit before I get into that. I always did like to put off the hard things, even with my homework in school, I'd get the easy stuff done first, spelling words and such, and then, last, ARITHMETIC, which near about made me rip my hair off my head. Lord have mercy. I would do that arithmetic homework mostly wrong and then I would fuss and fume and go and raid the larder. Never was a cookie bit so hard as when I had been working with those numbers that seemed like leering tricksters to me.

This thing I mean to tell you will be the most important thing in this letter, besides my telling you how much I love you. And I'll tell you what, I'm glad I'm not trying to say this thing to you in person because I'm not sure I could. Anyway, you would probably cover your ears like you used to do sometimes and say, Nope, I'm not listening, la la la. You could be stubborn as a hunting dog being told to lay off his prey when you wanted to be. But I hope you'll read it and think on it, Ruthie. I hope in that way that even from the other side I might still help you.

Flo hears a rapping at her door and goes to let Teresa McNair in. When she opens the door, Teresa looks at her and says, "Oh, you're tired. I'll come back."

"I'm not tired!" Flo says, then immediately corrects herself. "Well, I am a bit, but I still would like your company. Do I look awful? And here I put on lipstick and everything!"

"You don't look awful," Teresa says. "You just look a little tired." She holds up a wicker hamper. "I did bring dinner, though. What do you say we share it, and then I'll be on my way?"

"Have a seat at the kitchen table and I'll get everything ready," Flo says. "I want to hear all about your rascal cat."

"Nothing to get ready," Teresa says. "I've got it all in here. Tin picnic plates, botanical themed, if you please. Elegant flatware, plastic though it is. Drinks, too, if you don't mind lemonade."

"I don't know why anybody drinks anything else!" Flo says.

They sit down and Teresa pulls out a yellow casserole dish with white polka dots on it. "Macaroni and cheese," she says. "And I've got sliced tomatoes, and for dessert, some chocolate chip cookies I baked this morning."

"My goodness! I wish I'd met you before now!"

"I'm embarrassed I never introduced myself."

"Things get away from us," Flo says. "Speaking of getting away, how *is* your cat?"

"Well, I'll tell you," Teresa says, dishing out the food. "When I got home, I couldn't find him. He was on my back porch. I have no idea how he got out again. Nothing was left open!"

"Maybe you should name him Houdini," Flo says.

Teresa says, "Maybe I will. Although if I have to go outside to call him, it might be embarrassing to be yelling, 'Hou*di*ni!'"

Flo takes a bite of macaroni and cheese. "Oh, my goodness. This is just delicious!"

"Thank you. My mother's recipe. She said when she first made it for my dad, he called it 'Marryin' Mac 'n Cheese.' I guess it worked. They were happily together for just short of seventy years!"

She smiles at Flo, but it's a sad smile. "I've never married. That's why I got a cat. I was getting too lonely."

Flo looks up quickly at Teresa, who smiles and shrugs. "It's true."

Flo has always appreciated someone who leads with honesty and openness from the get-go, someone who doesn't wait to say things that they feel are important to say. One of her best friends, Gretchen Hardy, was a woman she met at a party who, after they exchanged names, said, "I have to tell you, parties make me terribly nervous. I might have to disappear into the bathroom a few times to collect myself." And Flo said that she felt nervous at parties, too, and asked would Gretchen mind if Flo joined her in the bathroom? Gretchen said certainly not, and that was it, they were close friends for many years.

And so now, feeling free to be honest herself, Flo says, "Huh, I would not have pegged you as being lonely. You seem so friendly and outgoing."

"I try to be. But lately the loneliness has gotten a bit more . . . *pronounced,* I guess I'd say."

"I see. Well, I'm sorry about that. Loneliness can be awful hard to bear. After my husband died—this was years ago—I thought I'd plum lose my mind from missing him. I have to say it never went away, completely. But now that I'm . . . Well, I won't have to worry about it much longer."

"How do you mean?"

Flo puts down her fork. "I've been given only a few weeks to live. My doctor just told me. I hadn't even been feeling that poorly, just losing a lot of weight, and feeling dizzy sometimes. Isn't it funny how you can have a thing raging in your body and be so unaware?"

Teresa sits very still, staring intently at Flo. Then she asks gently, "Do you want to talk about it? I'm a death doula."

"What's that?"

"We help people transition from life to death. Some call us death midwives."

"You don't say," Flo says, in what she hopes is a polite way, but she is thinking, *Death midwife!!* She looks out the kitchen window, where the clouds are pinkening with the sunset, and points to them. "Look at that," she tells Teresa.

Teresa looks out and says, "Beautiful. You know, I had a patient once tell me that the best index he had to his mental health was whether or not he looked up at the sky every day."

"I do have to say I wish I didn't have to go quite yet," Flo says. "Not just yet. But then I guess that's what everybody says to you."

"It depends," Teresa says. "Sometimes people are ready,

even more than ready. Other times they're not ready at all. One man I knew was terminal—he had been given just a couple of weeks, and he was sent to a hospice facility. He'd been a wonderful gardener; people used to come by his house just to stare at his flowers and vegetables. He told the staff he didn't mind dying so much, but he was worried about who would take care of his garden.

"Well, he lay around and waited. Waited some more. Days passed, then weeks, and finally he said, 'I have a proposition. Let me go home and garden some more and then I'll come back.' He moved out of hospice and back into his house. Got right back out in his garden. Two years later, his granddaughter found him sitting in front of his fireplace on a winter afternoon. He had passed away peacefully there."

"Isn't that something," Flo says.

Teresa leans forward slightly to ask Flo, "Do you believe in miracles?"

Flo shrugs. "I never really asked myself that question. But I guess I do. Seems like miracles abound, only usually we aren't paying enough attention." She gestures out the window again.

"I mean miracles like unexplained cures for illness," Teresa says.

"I've heard of that," Flo says, "only, with someone my age, seems like it might be unlikely. Not impossible! But unlikely."

"I always think that *will* has so much to do with it," Teresa says.

"Will who?" Flo asks, but she knows it's not much of a joke. She says, "I have heard of people making up their mind that this or that was or was not going to happen. One of these new wave things, I believe it's called—"

"New age?" Teresa says.

"That's it. They say you manifest something. I guess the idea is that if you just believe hard enough . . . Well, anyway, I may be old, but I am not too old to get me some daisies from the backyard to put on this table!"

Teresa smiles. "I'll help you pick some."

Flo goes to her cupboard for a certain dark blue vase, her daisy vase. "Wait till you see how perfect they look in here," she says.

After they gather daisies in the fading light, Flo puts them on the table and they eat the delicious cookies Teresa has brought—the old Mrs. Fields recipe, Teresa tells Flo. Then Teresa looks at her watch and says, "I'd best get back to Flash. That's what I decided to name him."

Teresa washes up her yellow casserole dish in the sink, dries it off, and then tells Flo, "I have a tradition where if I bring someone dinner, I gift them with the dish it came in. May I leave this for you?"

"Oh, my. Well, I do love the color yellow and I love polka dots, too. But are you sure you want to part with it? It's just as cheerful as can be. A kind of Kewpie doll of a dish, do you know what a Kewpie doll is?"

"I do. I'm older than I look."

"How old is that?"

"Fifty-one."

Teresa heads for the door, and Flo says, "Hold on. I believe I ought to give *you* a dish. I'm doing a little cleaning house. You know."

"I'll take a dish if you want," Teresa says. "But I think this might be the time when you tell yourself you are ready for your own miracle." She comes over to Flo and says quietly, "Close your eyes and think hard that you want your body to heal. Take it seriously." She takes Flo's hands into hers.

Flo closes her eyes. Then she pops them open. "Whooeee, I just felt something. A big rush of a feeling running straight up."

Teresa touches Flo's shoulder. "I'd love to visit you again."

"I hope you will. Any time."

Flo stands on the porch to watch the last of the colors leach from the sky. She has heard of people in California who gather together to watch the sunset like they'd watch a show. And they clap afterward! She wishes she'd have done that. That is something she should have done regularly. She thinks about how when you watch a sunset, the sun slips away so fast. Only at the end, though. You watch thinking it will last forever, but then the sun all of a sudden flattens, becomes a pinpoint of hard shining light with those holy rays, and then: gone.

Of course, nighttime has its charms. The hooty owls and the frogs singing and how a voice can carry. And if you're lucky the sky fills up with stars like to take your breath away no matter how old you are or how many times you've seen them. The stars can set you to wondering outside yourself, is the thing. They can make your mind big. No need to miss the sun if the stars come out right after.

Flo sits in the rocker and closes her eyes. She remembers when she was a girl and liked to sit out on a blanket in her backyard and watch the sunset most every night. She wrapped her arms around her knees and rested her chin on them and held still and watched. She always did say it was a full-out education, just watching. She's told people that's what she got her doctorate in, taking note of Homo sapiens and environs. One thing she loved about Terrence was how he never made fun of her lack of education, and so she learned. Just about anybody would learn if you gave them a running start of *I like you how you are already.*

After Flo washes up and gets into bed, she thinks about whether a mind might really be able to cure a body. She *had* felt that jolty feeling, and she had never felt anything like that in her life. But how much faith could someone have in something like that? She is ninety-two. Her doctor is not a dope.

She turns onto her side and closes her eyes, even though it's awfully early to go to sleep. Flo thinks one of the pleasures of living alone is that you can nap or go to bed whenever you feel like it. But when you wake up alone, doesn't the ticking of the clock sound so loud.

She lies still, thinking of the dinner she had with Teresa, and the way Teresa had brought everything in her hamper, even plastic cutlery. Flo should have suggested they use some of her fancy silver, which she ought to have used more often. This reminds her of something, and so she gets out of bed and goes downstairs to add a little more to her letter.

Ruthie, do you remember a collection of silver spoons, mismatched pieces I'd collected? You always liked them. I remember one summer day, the breeze pushing at the dining room curtains and you were lining those spoons up, making them spaced exactly even. You had graduated high school and were off to college the next day and you seemed sad about it. You had come over to say goodbye and it was lunchtime and I asked you if we should have a fancy goodbye lunch together, and by fancy I meant we'd eat tuna sandwiches in the dining room, and I'd cut off the crusts. I came out into the dining room with our plates and there you were, sitting before those spoons, and they had a silvery glow with the sun coming in on them. You looked up when I came in and you said how pretty the spoons were. This, too, seemed to make you sad. And then I remembered how you used to use those spoons for Terrence's soup when he was sick, when he got to where he couldn't hardly eat you liked to bring him soup with a different silver spoon every day. Well, look at this, he would say, every time. And you would sit by his bed while he ate and just talk to him. It was a kindness beyond what a child can usually offer, Ruthie. You did that.

But anyway, I was remembering that day when you'd lined the spoons all up. And I asked you, when we sat down to eat, were you okay. And you commenced to crying and said you wanted to go to college but you didn't want to go away. And then you started talking about how things could never be perfect and you always wanted them to be perfect. And you moved one of the spoons just a tiny bit to be in exact alignment. You looked up at me and said, See? And I remember just what I told you. I told you that part of life was learning how perfect imperfect could be. You just sighed but you thought about what I'd said, I know you did. That was one of the many times I wished I were your mother. I always wanted to be a mother, I wanted it awful bad. But year after year I would turn to Terrence on a certain day of the month and tell him my "friend" had come and he would nod and say quietly, All right. And then one day he said, It's just not for us, then, and that was the last we ever spoke of it. He never let on how much that particular loss hurt him. We contented ourselves with taking care of the neighborhood kids, which you know very well since we spoiled you nigh unto kingdom come.

Flo, Teresa, and Flash the cat are sitting on Flo's front porch in the early evening on Saturday night. A boy maybe ten years old comes to the bottom of the stairs. "Knock, knock," he says.

"Come in," Flo says, and the boy climbs up onto the porch.

"I'm just seeing if you need some help with your garden," he says. He hands Flo a flyer. The Wacky Weed Puller, he calls himself, and he charges ten cents apiece for the weeds. He takes PayPal because his dad helps him do that.

"That's a good service," Flo says. "How is it you learned about weeds?"

"Huh?"

"How do you know what to pull and what not to pull?"

"Oh!" the boy says. "Well, see, weeds are taller."

"Okay," Flo says. "I'll keep you in mind. If you decide to diversify and sell chocolate bars, I'll for sure buy one of those from you."

"What kind of chocolate bars?"

"Hershey with almonds."

The boy nods gravely. "Okay. *May*be." He hops down the steps and goes over to the next house.

"He'll think about those Hershey bars," Flo says. "I'll bet you he shows up tomorrow with a few and then I'll need to buy them all."

"You wouldn't have to buy them all," Teresa says.

"Oh, they freeze well."

"You're a generous spirit, Flo."

The women sit quietly for a while, and then Teresa says, "I have been thinking about how someone like me is regarded. A spinster, you know. An old maid."

Spinster! Flo thinks. Old maid! Oh, poor Teresa. She says, "I can't imagine that anyone would think of you that way."

Teresa shrugs. "I don't mind. It's what I am." She smiles, but Flo doesn't believe Teresa doesn't mind.

"Teresa, tell me. Are you unhappy?"

"Isn't everyone, sometimes?"

"I'm asking because of something you said. Are you unhappy about being alone?"

Teresa thinks for a moment. Then she says, "I resent the implication that a person has to be with another *person* to be happy."

"But people do seem to need each other. Would you agree with that?"

Teresa leans back in her chair. "You know what, Flo? I was in McDonald's the other day and there was a really old woman working there. She was clearing tables and wiping them down. And sometimes I wonder about what's going to happen to me when I get too old to do what I do, and I saw that woman and I thought, Well, I could do that. I wouldn't mind that job, wiping down tables, seeing what the people ate, listening in on the conversations that are going on. Plus I'd get a free lunch! I imagined where that woman might live; a small apartment, probably overheated, a nice chair to sit on, sliders onto a little balcony just loaded with plants, a lamp in the window. And—"

"Oh, Teresa," Flo says, shaking her head.

"It's not *sad,*" Teresa says. "I really wouldn't mind it. A job where you see people all the time, and you don't have to think too much. A job with a clearly defined beginning, middle, and end. No complications to think about when you get home. You live as you want to live."

"What about friends?" Flo asks. "Don't you think there's some value in having friends, at least?"

Teresa looks over at her. "Aren't we friends?"

"Well, yes, of course," Flo says. "But wouldn't you be happier coming home from your McDonald's job *to* someone?"

"I honestly don't know," Teresa says, and at that moment she seems to Flo to look just like a little kid.

Flo says, "I'm sorry. I don't mean to push you into *my* way of thinking."

"It's okay. Sometimes I . . ." She turns to face Flo more directly. "When I was growing up, all my friends had the same ideals for the man they would like to marry. Rich, handsome, witty . . . you know. But all I ever wanted was a man who was true."

Flo sighs. "Yes. But how do you ever know for sure?"

"Did you ever hear that saying, 'You can never know the whole man, but you can know the true man'?" Teresa asks.

"Never did hear that. What's it mean?" Flo shifts her position slightly. Her stomach hurts, but she doesn't want to tell Teresa. She wants to know the answer to the question she asked.

Teresa picks up Flash and puts him in her lap. She strokes the cat's back, long, slow strokes, and he closes his eyes. "I think it means you can never really get to the bottom of knowing a person," Teresa says. "There's so much inside each of us. But you can get a strong sense of certain fundamental qualities. You can come to a point of knowing *enough*. I guess what I wanted was a man with a sense of integrity. A willingness to share. And a kind of vulnerability."

"You talk like it's too late."

"It is too late."

"Oh, Teresa, it is not."

"It is!"

"You want to step outside and we'll settle this thing?" Flo asks, and a cloud of tension dissipates.

Flash hops down from Teresa's lap. He is wearing a little harness Teresa got for him that Flo thinks even he cannot escape. He has a leash on, too, and for some reason Flo finds this funny, and she laughs.

"What?" Teresa asks.

"A leash on a cat!"

"Laugh all you want to, it works," Teresa says. "Flash feels all *Born Free* and I have the security of knowing that he's not going to run off on me like every other man I've let into my life."

"Is that true?" Flo asks. "Has every man you've let in your life run off?"

"Well, maybe I've chased them off."

"Why would you do that?"

"Just beating them to the punch, I guess."

"What do you mean?"

"I know that eventually they'll realize . . . they'll find out things about me that they don't like." She looks down into her lap.

"What things?"

"Just . . . things."

"So, fear?" Flo says.

"No. Not really fear."

"Discomfort with commitment?"

"No, I don't think it's that, either."

"Maybe fear of happiness? I've met some people, seems like they think they don't *deserve* happiness. I never did understand that. But is that you, Teresa?"

"My goodness, Flo! I'm going to have to get you a shingle to hang outside!"

"Oh, I know. I guess some might say I'm a busybody. I'm sorry if I offended you. Let's us change the subject."

"No, we don't have to do that. It's just that some things are kind of embarrassing to admit. I don't think I'm ever going to have the kind of relationship you're talking about. Things just don't work out for me. But I really like talking to you, Flo. You seem like someone I might say anything to."

"You're right."

A weighty silence descends, and then Teresa speaks quietly. "I used to think a lot about suicide."

Flo cups a hand to one ear. "About . . . ?"

"Suicide."

Flo sits up straighter in her chair. "Oh, my."

"I'm not like that anymore," Teresa says.

"But you say you used to be?" Flo can hardly stand it. She wants to run over and embrace Teresa, to *shake* her, but she knows better than to do that. Let the woman talk.

Teresa sighs. "I've never told anyone this before, but when I was a freshman in college—this would be more than thirty years ago—I had a relationship fall apart. I'd been so *sure* of us. But he just abruptly broke up with me and I couldn't seem to get over it. My whole worldview changed. One night when I was feeling particularly sorry for myself, I got a bunch of aspirin and thought I'd . . . But then"—she looks over at Flo and laughs—"this will make it sound like I wasn't really serious. What I ended up doing was buying a pizza and eating the whole thing. And after that, things started to get better. Never underestimate the power of pepperoni.

"I think it's just that from the time I was a little girl, I was oversensitive to everything—I *felt* everything too much. By the time I was a teenager, I was sure I knew what life was all about and I figured it would only get worse. Then when I met what I thought was my true love, everything changed. The possibilities! The . . . *union* of us! The protection, the joy that the idea of all that brought! But then it fell apart, so easily, and I thought, Well, there you go. So much for trusting in love.

"But I feel now that it's beautiful to be alive. I've felt that way for a long time. I'm *okay* alone! I'm at peace with it. But that's enough about me. Tell me how *you're* doing. What have *you* been thinking about?"

What Flo wants to say is that she's been sitting here listening to Teresa and thinking that she is such a fine person, so deserving of so much more. But Teresa has signaled that she's had enough of talking about herself, at least for now, and so Flo turns the attention to herself. She says, "Well, I've been thinking I ought to pick out something nice to be laid out in."

"Oh?"

Flo straightens her glasses on her face and looks over at Teresa. "My friend Pris once invited me to her independent living place. Her name is Priscilla, but we all called her Pris from an early age because she *was* a prissy kind, always walking around with her nose in the air, stepping over mud puddles with a look of horror on her face, washing her hands rather than licking the frosting off them like the rest of us did.

"When I visited her last, we had a plateful of shortbread cookies with our coffee, and she told me she'd been thinking about what she would like to be laid out in, and she wasn't even sick! But there comes a time. She said, 'You know, I've got this turquoise negligee William gave me years ago. I only wore it but two or three times and it didn't stay on long, if you know what I mean. It was transparent, and when you put on the matching robe it was *still* transparent.' She winked at me and said, 'We liked that in those days, didn't we? But anyway,' she said, 'I was thinking, What if there is a heaven and you can arrive all young again and dressed in whatever you want? I would like to meet him dressed in that negligee he gave me. Do you think that's sinful?' I told her, 'No, I do not.' I said, 'In fact, you're giving me ideas for when my time comes.' Though I never did own such a thing as a negligee. It was not something Terrence and I could afford, a garment meant to dangle over someone; we were more practical. My nighties had lace and flowers, but that is not the same thing at all as what Pris was talking about.

"She took me into her bedroom, and in her dresser was that negligee, still wrapped in perfumed tissue, and it was like a cloud of a thing, a beautiful turquoise cloud, seemed like it had been spun by fairies."

Now the pain Flo is feeling increases. She shifts on her chair and pretends it is only so she can look out at the yard better. She stares straight ahead but continues with her story. "Pris asked if I would like for her to model it and then we laughed; she was only kidding, of course. But she wanted to be wearing it in case she transformed into that young Pris, and oh goodness, what a sultry young woman she was. Men turning their heads to watch her walk by, and sometimes it seemed like they might could have walked right into a brick wall. A *beautiful* woman."

The women sit quietly, and then Flo says, "What I want is to be buried in my travel suit, which I wore only once but always supposed I might use again. I felt as beautiful in it as I spect Priscilla felt in her negligee. I wore it on the one and only airplane ride Terrence and I ever took. He won an award from work and we went clean out to San Francisco, California, for a fancy vacation. Oh, that was something, and the plane ride out there was as good as anything we saw. When those propellers started turning, I felt like Ingrid Bergman in that hat she wore in *Casablanca*."

A sharp pain now, and Flo says, "Will you excuse me for a minute?"

She goes to the bathroom and stands there, and the pain subsides. Huh. Well, she's always had a rather delicate digestive system. Not like some others who seem like they can eat *any*thing. Terrence, for example, who could probably have salted an earwig, eaten it, and called it delicious.

Why don't you try to find *someone?* she wants to ask Teresa, which means, *Don't you* see *you?* But maybe Teresa can't see herself. Maybe no one can see themselves, really. Flo has heard about true mirrors, which show people the reverse image of what they usually see in mirrors: they let people see themselves as other people see them. But maybe other *people* are the real—and better—true mirrors.

There must be a way she can help Teresa. Someone she could ask some questions of. Wait a minute! Why not a librarian? They know everything. And they don't make you feel foolish, no matter what you ask.

I have a photograph of me in my bedroom in a red coat with big white buttons. There's a story behind that coat.

When I was nineteen years old, I had a job manning the counter at a dry cleaner called Tidy Press. Working at a dry cleaner was not on my lit-up bulletin board of the mind, but I figured it would do until something better came along. The people who owned it, Mr. and Mrs. Schmitt, were a study in contrasts. He was as nice as he could be, he was so kind. His wife, though. I always told my friend Judy McGrath that the wife reminded me of a coat hanger, all hard angles, skinny and stiff as could be. You've heard it said that some people are so unsmiling it seems like their faces would crack if they did smile. Mrs. Schmitt smiled all the time, but it was thin and vicious. Seemed like her favorite thing to do was to wait for me to do something wrong. She yelled at me for dropping things. For mispronouncing a customer's name. For not moving quickly enough. For moving too quickly. For dressing wrong. I didn't hardly know how to hold my head after a while. She chipped away at me. I remember one day I came home after work and called Judy and I was bawling on the phone so bad she could hardly make out what I was saying. But finally she said, Tell you what, come on over to my house and we'll go out for ice cream sundaes. Judy was pregnant then and she had a sundae just about every day. She said the baby demanded it, and I for one was glad it did. Well, we had a bolstering talk and the next day at work I went into the back to get some safety pins and when I came out Mrs. Schmitt started screeching about my leaving the counter unattended for the three seconds it took me to get the pins. She had my paycheck in her hand. I snatched it from her and then I said, I quit. Oh no you don't, she said. Oh yes I do, said I, right plucky, and I knocked on Mr. Schmitt's door and I told him thank you for hiring me and I sure did appreciate the work, but this would be my last day and goodbye. You know he didn't even ask me why. He knew. He said, You're a good girl. I said, Well, I'd always thought so. I wish you the very best, he said, going back to his ledger and his buzzing desk light, which he also put up with.

I called Judy to meet me at Woolworth's, and on the way I went to Ebert's department store, where I'd seen a red coat in the front window that I liked but it was too expensive for me. I guess you know the rest of the story. Every time I wore that red coat, I felt the strength of standing up for myself. When I sat down with Judy that day, she said, Nice coat, and I said, You don't know the half of it. I had enough money left from my paycheck to buy both our sundaes, and that's what I did. And don't you know I found another, much better, job the very next day. Seems like sometimes you say, I've about had enough, and something else says, Well, why didn't you say so, then. Here. And here. And here.

I guess I feel like this story might in a roundabout way help you some with your decision. Oh, Honey, don't you remember the time your whole family came to visit and you and your husband were standing out in my backyard while your children played Mother May I with me and I saw your husband put his hand to your cheek in a way so tender I had to put my hand to my own face. Ruthie, when you are recalling injustices, recall the other things, too.

Flo opens her refrigerator to contemplate what she might have for dinner. Nothing looks too appealing. She decides she'll just have cold cereal, something she likes a lot any time of day. Her friend Barbara Fanning used to tell her, "Flo, if you keep eating that you'll get big as a house; it's well documented." Anything Barbara wanted you to believe she would tell you was well documented. And if ever you got impatient and asked *where* it was well documented, she'd say, "Never mind."

As she eats, Flo reads the community newspaper. There's a story about a cat in a nursing home that lies on the beds of the people there who allow it to. Flo thinks it might be a comfort to have a cat on her bed. She always wanted a cat, but Terrence didn't like them. "No cats!" he would say, and then he had to go and make a face when he said it, to boot. Flo didn't get mad at Terrence very often, but sometimes they would fight about the no-cat rule. Well, Flo fixed him. She got porcelain cats and kept them on her dresser, a mother cat and two kittens. Siamese. Those were her cats. The mother's name was Tippy and the kittens were Spill and Chase.

A little kid might want those porcelain cats. They could pretend they were pets same as she did. Take them outside or bring them to school for show-and-tell. A kid might break them but that's all right, they would have gotten broken from being used, which is entirely different from when you accidentally knock something off a table and there it is, gone forever, and you stand there staring hard at the broken thing like a certain look could bring all the pieces back together.

Do they still have show-and-tell in school? Flo wonders. She always liked seeing what other kids found interesting or special. One time when it was show-and-tell in her fourth-grade classroom, she had forgotten to bring something. So she took off her cardigan sweater, which had jewels at the shoulder, and when it was her turn she held it up and talked about it, told how her aunt had given it to her and it made her feel queenly. Well, the boys didn't care one whit, but some girls wanted to try that sweater on at recess. Flo was popular that day.

Schools do still have recess, at least. When Flo walks around the neighborhood, she passes an elementary school, and when it is recess time she always likes to watch and see what's going on. There's an awful lot of this so-called technology that Flo finds mostly incomprehensible; she is not one of those modern older women wearing stylish sneakers and poking at a little telephone screen. *Everybody* is poking at their screens except for animals! Even toddlers. Not long ago, Flo saw a woman pushing a toddler in a carriage and they were *both* on their phones. Flo had to stop walking and stare. And she knows other people's business is not her business but heavens to Betsy.

One thing Flo likes about watching recess is that it's still the same. No technology out there, leastwise not yet. Just kids hanging by their knees from the jungle gym or riding high on the swings, or big groups of kids chasing each other at breakneck speed and yelling their heads off, or maybe a couple of kids huddled together in the corner of the playground hatching a plot or pretending something. Once she heard a little boy say, "Let's play Army and have names. I'll be Colonel Bill Williams." "Bill and William are the same thing," said one of his friends, and the little boy said, "No they are not. One is Bill and one is William."

In Flo's opinion, pretending is awfully good for you. It can lift you up and take you miles away from where you are. And of course kids are natural actors, and don't they *become* a cat, or a monster with seven eyes waving around on stalks, or a king in some made-up land. Occasionally she sees a little kid alone, maybe wearing glasses with an elastic round the back of his head, maybe dragging a stick behind him. Flo likes to chance talking to kids like that, leaning over the chain-link fence to holler yoo-hoo and ask how they're doing. She always wants to share some butterscotch candies from her purse with them but Lord knows you can't do *that* anymore. But she asks how they're doing. And because they are children and have trust and willingness and honesty, they will usually tell her. And mostly they are fine, just solitary beings who like to think their own thoughts. Flo always thinks, Well, there's another Steve Jobs coming up.

I still have that little table and chairs you used to sit at to color, or to make your paper fortune tellers. Do you remember how you used to put some bad fortunes in there sometimes? "A truck will mow you down" was one. I told you once you ought not to do that, and didn't you look me straight in the eye and say, Life is not all fun and games, Flo. What were you, eight or nine? I nearly busted out laughing, but instead I just nodded and said I guess not, but I'm going to hope I don't get a fortune like that too often! And you patted my hand and said, Now, Flo, you won't.

I hope you won't throw away that table and chairs, Ruthie. I'm sure some child can use them, and you know children are always so pleased when furniture fits them.

Don't throw away my cast-iron skillet, either. It is so well seasoned now, everything you cook in it tastes good. My daddy used it for fried chicken that made you want to beat your fists on the table. I saw how he made it, but mine never turned out as good as his so that is one recipe I will not be giving you. But if you can eat in heaven guess what I'm ordering to accompany my mound of mashed potatoes big as Mount Kilimanjaro and two ears of corn plucked straight from the field.

Do you know the best way to cook corn on the cob? Put it in a pan of cold water with a squeeze of lemon and a pinch of sugar. Bring it to a boil and let it go two minutes, then turn off the flame and let it set for ten. Bingo.

I'll tell you what, there's nothing wrong with serving just corn on the cob and sliced tomatoes for dinner in summertime. Go out to Dairy Queen afterward and sit at their picnic table and eat your ice cream and watch everybody else eat theirs and you will have had yourself a day.

Speaking of eating, I just remembered a time I watched you eat a tablespoon of dirt, and when I asked you what in the world you were doing you said you were seeing how it tasted plus you were not afraid of germs. You must have been about seven, sitting out in my front yard under the Miss Kim lilacs, which was one of your favorite places where you sometimes made little houses complete with crops, which were red berries you lined up straight in rows. That day you ate dirt, you had one eye squinted against the sun and you were wearing the cutest yellow sundress with spaghetti straps that I figured you'd begged your mother for but then had sullied by nine that morning—jelly stains and mud and butterfly dust. What a fierce little girl you were, fierce and gentle all at the same time. I had a good laugh remembering your eating dirt.

I woke up today to a rose-gold-colored morning and it was the prettiest day, the kind where the world seems washed, everything about as crystal clear as it gets, even to these old eyes. The lines of the roof on the house across the street, the little bend of the twig on the tree when a bird landed on it, so sure of himself and looking around in that proprietary way birds can have. Well, I got dressed and went out on the porch and sat down on my wicker chair with the cushions so old I don't remember how old, but they are comfortable, they know me and my bones. I sat there and I had the sharpest feeling of sorrow that I would be leaving all this soon, the common wonders of the world.

And then you know, I just got afraid. I got afraid in that way of when you might look all right on the outside but on the inside you feel the trembling. And I got up and despite the glory of the day I got back in bed and lay real still. I was thinking, What can I do, what can I do? I closed my eyes and pulled my breath seems like down to my toes, and I said to myself, I shall be released.

Only problem with that is I don't want to be released, not today, not with the sun carving out a living painting right before my eyes. Not with the way I want to help my new friend Teresa. It seemed like I was going to go into a panic, maybe crying and thrashing around and the like, and there I was all dressed with even my shoes on. Well, I got up and I straightened the bed and I went outside again fast as I could, went around to the backyard, where I stood beside the clothesline pole and I asked myself this question: Do you want to hang out yet another load of laundry when you can't hardly lift a towel? Haven't you hung out enough wash in all your years? Here came the answer whooshing into my heart: No. I wouldn't mind a bit hanging up a few more loads, and if you're one of those never saw the point in hanging out pillowcases, I'll hang yours for you, and when they're dry I'll deliver them to you come twilight and say rest your head on these when you go to bed and smell the sunshine, even with the darkness come and the wind blowing. Close your eyes and turn your face to that smell and you will feel cared for like when your momma yanked your blankets clean up to your chin and planted a kiss on your forehead that you will forever long for. And someone else can kiss you on the forehead but it's not the same, lovely as it might be, it's not the same.

Well, now look how I am going on about that, I wonder if I am plum going to lose my mind. I hope not. I got to sniff and center here, and that's what I did out in my backyard, finally, I did sniff and center, it's something I've done forever to calm down. I close my eyes and take long breaths and go down into myself deep and still. And on that day I also closed my eyes and made cups of my hands and I prayed to Jesus to fill me with light and help me not to be afraid. And it worked. Lot of people don't ask Jesus for anything, thinking He has got a long checklist and they don't hardly figure in it. But I don't believe that's how it works, to me Jesus just waits for us to call on Him, and then it's just as likely as not He'll gather you in His arms and your prayer will be answered. It happens! Naturally I don't mean He really gathers you in His arms, you just feel like that, cared for, and heard. Terrence never did buy any of that religion stuff (he called it crap, which always made me so fearful that here would come a lightning bolt for us both), but he never tried to take my faith from me. He would shake his head gentle, but he never said one unkind word about my beliefs. Terrence was just more practical. For him, life was in and out. In and out. I suppose if you keep that in your head, it offers a certain strength. But Ruthie, the light this morning.

Let me move on. Here is something I am right embarrassed about. In the top drawer of my breakfront in my dining room you will find just about a million candles. Over and over again I would splurge on long, elegant tapers and then I would find them too pretty to burn. Oh, I used candles, but only the cheap ones. The pretty ones stayed in the drawer where no one could see them. Now, a candle's flame is pretty no matter what, but I hope you will use those long candles. Maybe you could do like in romantic movies and burn them all at once. Wouldn't that be pretty?

Now, the china I did use. But I was nervous, doing it. Something could break. And you know what? Nothing ever broke. Nothing. And what if it had?

Long as I'm doing embarrassing confessions, I want to tell you about a certain cake stand I have. It is green and has a floral imprint pattern and I used it for cake when company came.

I used to get right nervous when company came, and I never could overcome that demon. I would fuss about everything, it like to drove Terrence out of the house every time we were having people over for dinner. I wouldn't let him help, you see. I would say JUST LET ME DO IT! mean as a snapping turtle. So he'd maybe run some errands or go out on the porch and I'd fuss and fuss. And I'd put the cake I made on the stand and sometimes I even lined flowers around the edge and still it didn't make me happy because I worried were the flowers okay. I tell you, it was awful, for years I was that way! Most of my life I was that way! I wanted to invite my dear friends over, and I would visualize us all around the table, talking and laughing and everyone enjoying their food. But when the day came it all seemed like too much work for me, my blood felt like sludge in my veins, and I would wish I could go away and send in my double to take the reins. She could take the reins and I could set out on the porch and listen to the birds sing. The reason I am telling you this is to say if you are like this you'd best try to stop now while you are still young. Don't say,

Oh, I wonder if they will say something bad if I sprinkle a bit of sugar on the sliced tomatoes. You just go ahead and sprinkle the sugar. It's your house. They've come for dinner. Enjoy them. And enjoy yourself. You might could use that cake stand. It does set things off. And there wasn't a one didn't remark on how pretty the flowers looked when I did up the cake that way.

Honestly. The years we spend worrying about not much. It's truly years. Decades! I wonder why when we get to the end, we so often pull all the years we've lived through up close for a look-see and then like to smack our foreheads. The saving grace is all the things we do right. Taking a hand needs holding. Offering an apology when one is sorely needed. Stopping to watch or listen or be steeped in gratitude, oh you know how that can happen, I once watched a toddler go in and out of a playground fountain with her little pink swimming suit on, ruffles at the butt. And her diaper hanging low. And she was a little afraid but mostly exhilarated. I had to sit on the bench and watch a while. And all the way home, I felt like watching that child had let me build a little chapel inside myself, and I'd watched that little girl like she was a living prayer. Maybe she was.

Well, I'm fixing to make dinner and I guess I'll have me some hard-boiled eggs. Which reminds me of something else I want to tell you about.

Flo has always loved that her neighborhood is near the little branch library. It's no more than a five-minute walk from Flo's house, and she decides she'll go there today to ask some questions of the librarian that might help with Teresa.

She puts on a black dress with blue flowers, one of her favorites, never mind the fraying on the edge of one side of the belt. She'll bring a cardigan for when she goes into the library; it might be cold in there. Seems like people think they ought to roast you to death in the winter and freeze you to death in the summer.

She walks down her front steps and turns right and for a few moments she forgets about everything but the task at hand. And look how well she's walking, not out of breath, a steady pace. If a stranger passed, he wouldn't know a thing other than she was an old lady out for a walk. She could go into a dimestore and buy something, she could go to a movie, she could order a cup of soup at a diner. She could still do those things. But today she is going to the library.

Outside of Mildred Curtis's house, Flo sees the screen door opening and here Mildred comes down her porch steps. Mildred is someone whom Flo probably should have been friends with, but never was—maybe the age difference; Mildred is a good ten years younger. But Mildred is also a former actress who lived in New York City when she was young, and that always made Flo feel nervous around her. Still, Mildred's voice gentled you down, she had a calm and kind way of speaking. Her eyes held a great curiosity, too, and it seemed like whatever you were telling her was made more interesting just because of the way she stared so intently at you while you were telling the story. It made you want to add details—Mildred was in no hurry, that's the way she always was.

Mildred waves at Flo, holds up a finger, and comes over to her. Even in her eighties, Mildred is still so attractive, like a woman in a painting with her pretty skin and clear blue eyes, and she's kept her hair the original light brown color. No extra weight on her, either; Flo guesses she might be one of those who drives around with a yoga mat in the backseat of her car.

"I haven't seen you for the longest time," Mildred says. "It seems like it's harder than ever these days for people to get together. But I'm so happy to run into you, because I'm dying to tell someone about something that happened."

"Really! Well, invite me up onto your porch and tell me."

"Actually, I'd love to have you come inside. I just pulled a gingerbread out of the oven. Would you like some gingerbread with lemon sauce?"

One of Flo's favorite desserts, but she's particular about it. "Well, I'll tell you true. I love gingerbread, but only if it's got pepper in it. Do you put pepper in yours?"

Mildred puts her hand on her hip. "Do I put pepper in gingerbread? Of course I do!"

Flo follows Mildred into her bright yellow kitchen and sits at the Formica table. "Coffee?" Mildred asks, and Flo says that would be lovely.

The women enjoy a few bites of gingerbread—Flo has to admit it's wonderful—and then she asks Mildred, "So what happened?"

"Well. I just received a *check* in the mail. Because I am going to be published in a magazine!" Mildred sits back in her chair, her chin raised. "You know Lake McAllister, right?"

Flo knows it well, though it has been a long time since she's been there. It is less than a mile way, and it was always pleasant walking around that lake in the summer—wouldn't take but half an hour to circle the whole thing—and there were the willow trees at the edge dipping their leaves in the water and the ducks resting in the cool shade beneath the branches. Swans came, too, and one afternoon when Flo had taken little five-year-old Ruthie for a walk there, a swan had rushed out of the water and bit Ruthie's ankle. Ruthie hollered bloody murder and nothing would do but that her mother put a huge bandage on her when she got home when she hardly needed it, it was just a little red mark.

"Sure, I know that lake," Flo says. "Pretty over there."

"Do you remember that in the middle of the lake there are two islands, Twin Islands, they're called? They're pretty close together, a channel in between."

"Yes. Folks like to swim back and forth between them."

"Well," Mildred says, "this last winter I ice skated around those islands."

Flo looks at her. Blinks.

"You *ice skated* around them?"

"Yes, I did. And it was so special I wrote about it, and then I thought what I wrote was pretty good so I sent it to *Retiree* magazine, and they're going to publish it. And they paid me three hundred dollars! I just got the check today."

"That's wonderful!" Flo says, but she is thinking Mildred is plum crazy, ice skating at her age.

"I didn't fall down once," Mildred says, as though reading Flo's mind. "The lake had frozen and then it rained, and it froze again, smooth as glass—the surface was like a mirror. I'd driven past it earlier and then that night I was lying in my bed and I thought, I have to go and skate on it. I have to. I got my skates from the basement storeroom and off to the lake I went. Not a soul was there—well, it *was* one in the morning. But it was so quiet, and the stars so piercingly clear. I sat down on a bench and laced up my skates and then I made my way onto the ice. It was just perfect, like they make it for the hockey players. I skated out to the islands and circled them twice and then I came back to the shoreline and took off my skates and walked home. I felt like I was buzzing, almost like I had wings inside me going at a furious rate." She looks over at Flo and laughs. "Don't look so shocked! It was fine! I still have strong ankles and I was always a very good skater when I was young. I thought, When will it ever happen again that the ice will be like that? In my lifetime, I mean."

"How old are you, now?"

"Eighty-two, but you know what? When I was out there, I simply forgot my age. The only thing in my mind was the urge to skate again, under perfect conditions no less, and it seemed like everything was in harmony with me—the night sky and the ragged little dark clouds, the *skritch skritch* sound of my blades and fine spray of ice, the curlicue tracks I left behind like I was writing a love letter to the lake. I just had to do it! And it will be one of those memories that feels encased; we don't get so very many like that."

Flo nods. "You're right. And I think that story you just now told me is beautiful. When I was listening, it's like I was watching you in a movie."

Flo looks up at the kitchen clock then, and Mildred says, "Oh, I've kept you from where you were going. Let me wrap some gingerbread up for you to have later. Can you carry it all right?"

"Course I can. I'll put it in my purse."

Mildred wraps up the gingerbread and puts a little ribbon around it. "There!" she says. "Let me walk you out."

When they reach the sidewalk, Mildred says, "You know, I think sometimes when we age, we forget that we must keep on making new memories, keep on meeting new people and having new experiences. Seems like a lot of older people give up and spend all their time looking in the rearview mirror, when here is life still before them. I don't ever want to do that. I still want to do everything I can. I hope I get to have a *romance* again."

Flo smiles. "I hope you do, too, and then I hope you'll tell me another story, about *that.*"

"You'll be the first. But Flo, selfish me, I didn't even ask how *you* are."

Flo hesitates, then says, "I'm doing okay."

"You look a little tired."

"I am, I guess."

"Well, call me when you're rested, and we can think about doing something together."

"I will."

"I mean it!"

"I do, too."

Flo waves goodbye and heads for the library, more certain than ever of what she wants to do.

At the library, there is a line at the circulation desk, six people deep. Flo sits in a chair at a nearby table to wait.

She thinks it was nice, hearing the story Mildred told. It reminds Flo of times when Terrence went fishing with friends and came home and told her about it. At such times it was as though Flo were sitting beside Terrence in the gently rocking boat, the line cast out. It was as though she could hear the men talk in low voices as they waited for the tug on the pole that would mean supper. She would think about the sun warming the flannel of Terrence's shirt against his bent back, and she could almost hear the *lap, lap, lap* of the little waves against the hull. Flo loves books, but storytelling out loud is a wonderful thing, and she hopes people never forget how to do it.

The desk is free now, and Flo goes over to it. The middle-aged librarian sitting there is wearing some oversized black glasses that Flo thinks must weigh heavy on her nose.

"I'm sorry for the wait," the librarian says. "What can I help you with?"

"I have a computer question."

The librarian looks across the room and stands. "Let me take you over while we have one free. You can show me what you're having trouble with." She walks quickly over to secure the machine and Flo follows more slowly.

When the women are sitting before one of the computers, Flo feels like she's entered the inner sanctum of NASA. Next to them is a young man wearing headphones and tapping furiously away. Images appear, disappear, and change so rapidly it makes her dizzy.

"I don't really know how to use a computer," Flo whispers.

"That's okay, I can help you," the librarian says. "I'm Mimi, by the way."

"Florence. Well, *Flo*."

Mimi smiles at her and starts punching keys. She's wearing dangly silver earrings, which Flo looks at rather than the screen.

"Okay," Mimi says. "We're in. What's your question?"

"Well, it has to do with computer dating."

"Uh-huh."

"I want to know a little about it."

"All right. Is this for you, then?"

Flo laughs loudly, then covers her mouth. She still thinks that you're meant to be *quiet* in a library, all evidence to the contrary notwithstanding.

"*No,* it's not for me!"

The librarian raises her eyebrows and looks over at Flo.

"It's *not*!" Flo says.

"Oh, I believe you, it's just that it's not so out of the ordinary for mature people to want to use these sites."

"I'm ninety-two!"

The librarian leans in so close Flo can smell her shampoo. She says, "Yesterday I helped a ninety-five-year-old gentleman get on Match.com. He was looking for a lady companion."

"Ninety-five!"

Mimi nods. "Yup."

"Do you think he'll actually get a *date* out of it?"

"I think it's entirely possible that he will!"

"Well, that's hard to visualize, but honestly, I'm asking for a friend who thinks it's too late for her. There's not a thing wrong with her, she's lovely, just lacks confidence."

"How old is she?"

"Only fifty-one."

Mimi throws up her hands.

"I know," Flo says.

"I'm fifty-*three* and I'm out there. It's not too late for her!"

"I *know* it. So I thought maybe if I gave her some information about one of these date places, she might try it."

Mimi takes one of the slips of paper in a holder on the table and starts scribbling furiously, furrows between her eyebrows. "I'll write down the names of some dating apps that I think are pretty good. She might already know them. Mostly what she needs to know is that she has nothing to lose by going on. She doesn't have to accept any invitations, but it can help her confidence just to get some responses."

"Some *hope*!" Flo says, with such emphasis that her bottom rises up from the chair.

Mimi smiles over at her. "Exactly." She writes down three suggestions, folds the paper over, and hands it to Flo. "Good luck," she says. "You're kind to do this for your friend."

Flo starts to get up but then asks Mimi, "I hope it's not rude to ask you, but have you ever tried any of these things?"

"I have."

"And?"

Mimi shrugs. "Honestly? So far it's just . . . meh."

"Oh."

"But I'm going to keep trying."

"Good for you."

Flo tucks the paper into her purse. At the right time, she'll give it to Teresa. She'll say even the librarian does computer dating. She'll leave out the "meh" part.

One time early in our marriage, I took the train to see my mother. Terrence and I could hardly stand to be separated in those days, not like in later years when he would disappear into his workroom or I would take much too long looking at jam at the grocery store. I wonder do you remember, Ruthie, when you brought your fiancé to meet me, both of you pleased as punch that you had found your true love that was going to last forever and YOU two wouldn't EVER fuss at each other? Well, fussing is part of a marriage, just like hard times are part of a life. They help form it. You may not like it when it's happening, but you get through it and then you look back and say well fine then. Now I know something.

Speaking of fussing, listen to this one. One time Terrence and I had a fierce disagreement before bed. It was about the thing I'll tell you about later. I thought he and I had discussed it and put it to rest. But you know sometimes when you think you're all done with something, it rears up again. They say you shouldn't go to bed angry, but we were sure enough headed that way. I was muttering into my mirror while I took cold cream off my face. I thought, Tell you one thing, I am not sleeping with that man tonight. And off I went to the guest room, and I lay down in that narrow bed and I felt smug pleased with myself. So there! I was thinking, as I fell asleep. But I woke up some hours later and I reached my hand over and there was nothing. And I remembered where I was and I thought, For heaven's sake, go to your own bed and lie beside your husband. Well, I went to my bed and lo and behold it wasn't even turned down. I crept downstairs and there I found Terrence asleep on the sofa halfway falling off it, and the afghan pulled up tight in his fists. Terrence, I said, and his eyes popped open and he looked scared. Come to bed, I said, and I was speaking gentle, I could see he'd been startled hard. He sat up and blinked and then he said, Oh. I thought you were an angel. I am, I said, and I held out my hand and he took it and we ascended the staircase together.

But for heaven's sake I still haven't said about the hard-boiled eggs. My mind does wander.

So as I said, I once took the train to see my mother and before I left Terrence said, How about I make you some hard-boiled eggs to take on the train. I said that would be wonderful and I meant it because every time I see someone eat a hard-boiled egg on public transportation, I think, Well, weren't they smart.

Terrence saw me off at the station and come about lunch time I opened my paper sack. On the shell he had drawn a heart with an arrow through it and our initials inside, like you see carved into a tree. That made me have a private smile. But also he had taken a tiny little jar and put holes in the lid and there I had my own personal salt shaker. When someone thinks of things like this, you just feel so well cared for. Look what I got, I felt like saying to everyone, but naturally I kept it to just me. Which was enough. That little salt shaker is in the cupboard next to the bowls. It can still come in right handy.

It's only six o'clock, Ruthie, but I'll go to bed after dinner, you know there is a kind of luxury in going to bed early. I'll look at my ladies' magazine and then drift off. I do have some more things to tell you about. Seems like there's nothing like a reminder that your time is nigh to make you awfully talkative. I hope you'll be patient with me.

Flo wakes in deepest darkness. No moon. And she feels afraid.

She sits up and turns on the bedside light, pushes a pillow behind her, and begins rocking quickly back and forth, back and forth, something she hasn't done for the longest time. Arms crossed and holding on to each other, her eyes squeezed shut. She can feel her heart racing and it occurs to her to call her doctor. But that wouldn't be fair. It's the middle of the night and he wouldn't be able to do anything; it was only a bad dream. A terrible, terrible dream about the devil. She had gone to hell and here came the devil striding up to her, and he was red, with horns and cloven hoofs and a tail just like in the pictures, and he was walking all bowlegged up to her. He had a thin-lipped grin on his face that was terrifying, and behind him were high fires burning and black smoke rising and the poor souls crying out.

"Florence Greene?" he said, in a mocking voice that chilled her bones, and her throat wouldn't work to answer. She tried, but she felt paralyzed, and here he came closer and closer.

Now she is awake, breathing fast, and her frilly nightside lamp isn't doing much to help. She starts to sing her favorite hymn, "Do Not Be Afraid," but stops. It's no good, her trembly old voice against the shadows in the corners of the room. She thinks of Terrence and how he never did believe in hell *or* heaven. He always said that it was plain conceited for people to think they went on after they died. Flo would bristle every time, because she *wanted* there to be a heaven.

"What would we even *do* there?" Terrence asked her once. And Flo said, "What do you *mean*? We would be in *heaven*!" "Yes," he said, "but what would we *do*?" Flo said she guessed that for one thing they would visit with everyone up there, all the people they'd been missing so hard—there they would be. And maybe they would look down on Earth, too. They could watch what was happening there. Anywhere they wanted to watch, they could. She did not add that she imagined them sitting on the edge of a turquoise and pink cloud, holding hands and swinging their legs.

"Would we eat in heaven?" Terrence asked.

"Well, I spect so," Flo said.

"What would we eat?" he asked, and Flo knew he was kind of funning with her, but she went right along and said they would eat whatever they wanted. "Hm," said Terrence. "So we snap our fingers and here comes some fried chicken with buttermilk biscuits floating right over to us?"

Flo got impatient with him then and said, "You can make fun of me all you want, Terrence, but I got to believe in heaven."

"*Why?*" he asked. And Flo said, "Because it's our reward. Don't we suffer in this world? Don't some of us suffer so bad? It's our reward! And I also have to believe because if I lose you, why, in heaven I'll see you again."

He'd had a toothpick in his mouth that day, Flo remembers; they were sitting out on the porch on a lovely summer evening after a real good dinner of barbecued ribs, and he had a toothpick in his mouth, and he took it out to say serious to her, "All right, Flo, if you believe in heaven, that's okay with me. I won't make fun of it ever again. Do you believe in hell, too?"

She told him, "Yes I surely do and I hope I don't go there. You never know. You might think you're a good person and then on Judgment Day you find out something different. I'm sore afraid of the devil. I am afraid of even thinking of him."

"Put him in diapers," Terrence said.

Flo said, "What?"

Terrence said, "Whenever you think of the devil, imagine him in diapers."

Flo did that right on the spot; she conjured an image of the devil, and wasn't he wearing an old cotton diaper with great big safety pins on either side, and if you thought about it, those safety pins would be right hot. But Satan looked ridiculous, all his fury and hatred reduced by a saggy diaper.

And so that's what Flo does now: she thinks of the devil in his diaper, and she starts to laugh and she isn't afraid anymore and she whispers, "Terrence," and reaches out to his side and caresses his pillow. And all inside her it goes calm and quiet.

Then she remembers something. She turns on the bedside lamp and gets up and goes downstairs to find her little sewing basket that she keeps under the side table—Ruthie used to like to play with that basket; she lined up spools of thread and called them her soldiers. Flo finds the big safety pin in there so that if ever she fears the devil again, it will remind her of what to do. When she starts to come back upstairs, something peculiar happens. She can't move her legs to climb. But finally she makes her way up and is glad no one sees her practically crawling up the stairs. Why, she is embarrassed in front of her own self.

But the safety pin is now in her nightstand drawer. She'll have to tell Ruthie about it, what it means, how it changes terror into laughter, and if that isn't a good magic trick, Flo doesn't know what is.

She turns off the light and lies down again. She thinks about how she loved Terrence on the day she met him, and she knew right away she would love him all her life. Right away! She never would have predicted that he would be taking care of her long after he was gone. Yet he is. And she doesn't want to believe in the devil, but she sure does want to believe in heaven, and that she'll see Terrence again there. When it comes to Terrence, a lifetime was not enough. Forever won't be, either.

Do you remember how I used to tell you our stories, Ruthie? I just made things up and you listened to me like I was the pope on the Vatican balcony. One summer day just after you'd turned five you rang my doorbell and said, Flo, can you come out on the porch and tell me a story? Sure enough, I said, and we settled ourselves into the wicker chairs and I said what would you like a story about? Pizza, you said. Pizza! said I. You nodded all serious so I got serious too and I said all right, here is a story called The Lonely Little Pizza.

I started telling it out and then your face changed and you said, I have to go home and poop but after I poop can I come back and you tell me the rest of the story? Of course, I said, and I watched you climb down real careful off that chair which was too big for you and you had bandaids on your knees criss-cross from a recent mishap. But you climbed down careful and then you ran hell bent for leather over to your house and you slammed open the screen door and yelled real loud, MOM I GOT TO POOP AND THEN FLO IS GOING TO TELL ME THE REST OF HER STORY ABOUT THE LONELY LITTLE PIZZA. Well, who wouldn't love you, Ruthie?

In a box marked "Ruthie" up in the attic you will find drawings from before you could write. One of those drawings was you as a bride. And oh I just remembered one letter that you sent when you were in college. You said all the girls on your dorm floor ever talked about was how not to get pregnant. You said you had no interest in that since you were certainly not going to give it away. But then you changed your mind right quick and when you came home at Christmas break you and I took a walk around the block and you confessed to me that you had had sex and did I think that was bad, sex before marriage. I said I didn't think so, so long as you were both careful with each other, and that was a big relief to you.

Then (and I wonder if you will recall this) then you told me about your roommate going out with a boy she really liked for the first time. It was a chilly fall day and they were in his car and she passed gas. And she told you she quick rolled down the window and acted like she just needed some air but unfortunately it was too late. That incident kind of spoiled the mood and he never did ask her out again and she felt real bad because she thought he would always associate her with farting. You wanted to know did I think that was fair. I said well of course not. You said I don't think so either. But then we both busted out laughing. Oh poor Kay, you said.

You sent me letters about jobs you had after you graduated, and then about Jonathan, including after your first date with him when you said you thought you'd met The One. And you told me he was real precise the way he cut up an apple for the two of you to share and you liked that. You told me he had the gentlest touch and was quick to smile and was patient and a good listener. I remember thinking, My, she's found a good one. Course your most recent letters talk about your frustrations with him and your thoughts about divorce and that hurts me bad Ruthie and I'm sure it hurts you two as well. I guess you can't have a marriage without hurt and you'll surely see what I mean when I tell you about what happened between Terrence and me, that secret I kept for so long.

But that day when you were little and I was telling you the story I had to quick think of why a pizza might be lonely, but I did it. Children make you think of things you never would have thought you could conjure up, don't they? You would know now, having children of your own. And now I've got to just go and set a spell and think about your children who will be steamrollered if you do go through with it. Divorce. I don't mean to make you feel bad, I'm just telling you my true and whole feelings, like we always have.

Flo is sitting in the living room looking out the window at the rain. She took a short walk before the storm started and was charmed by a collection of toys some child had put at the base of a tree. It was almost like a deconstructed dollhouse. Flo saw that in one room, there were two figures standing face-to-face, as though engaged in serious conversation. One was a purple bear wearing a sundress and a red ribbon on top of her head. No shoes, Flo was happy to see. Keep a link to being wild! The other was an angel, white wings, white robe, and even white hair.

Flo stared at the two figures for a long time. She thought it was so interesting that a child would think of this, something recognizable from Earth talking to something representing that other realm, one that is unknown but that is nonetheless depended upon by so many.

She remembered the time after that terrible secret about Terrence was revealed, and they talked about what it had meant when it happened, and they talked about what it meant now, and Flo thinks they were both aching and afraid. But they were talking. And after they fell silent, Flo made up a movie in her head about going to an empty church and sitting in a pew and staring up into the face of a statue of the Virgin Mary, asking for help in making a decision. And she got help. Maybe it was from the Virgin Mary. Maybe it was from her own self. But she got help.

Now the rain stops, and the sun comes out. A million rainbows. She thinks of Ruthie, and she thinks of Teresa, and she thinks of all she might still have time for, and she is happy.

After Terrence died and I finally felt like eating again, I used to set myself up fancy. Now, by fancy I mean using dishes with personality. A heavy coffee mug with a green stripe around the top, that was Terrence's cup. And I found some coffee mugs in a thrift store years back that ended up being *my* cups. They are Mr. Rooster and Mrs. Hen. On the hen cup, there is a little baby chick round the other side. Oh, it's sweet, just pecking at the ground. I wonder if the artist had the hen all done and then got a little twinkle in their eye and thought hold on, I'm going to put a surprise on here. You will find those chicken mugs near the front of the cabinet on account of I use one just about every day.

What else. All the ironed napkins I have folded in the drawer of the dining room buffet, I don't guess you'd want them. If you don't iron them they look like they're fresh out of the rag bag, but it seems like no one irons anymore. It's funny how that happens, things falling out of favor, and these days to hell with wrinkles in your clothes, no one cares. No time to iron, everybody says, who has time to iron?

I had time. I moistened the clothes, I used a coke bottle with a sprinkler top, and then I rolled them and put them in the refrigerator in a plastic bag. Come time to iron, I turned on the radio to Arthur Godfrey for those years when he was on, and I set up the board by the window for double entertainment. Wouldn't sit down to iron ever, still don't, though the only thing I iron now is my pillowcases and hankies. I don't guess people want to iron cloth napkins, maybe they don't even use them. But maybe you could at least have a look at them before you pass them by, the pretty colors and the lace. Some have birds or flowers and some you'll see are only for Christmas.

I'm thinking if it comes that I can't stay here, if I have to go somewhere, I hope it will be a hospice place. I understand they are not so afraid of dying in those places, and they have windchimes in the trees outside the building and candles in the lobby and people will come to your room and strum on guitars for you. And also they will read aloud to you, which would be my pick. Read me a story and I'm not hardly here anymore.

"Am I disturbing you?" Teresa asks.

"Not at all," Flo says, opening the door wider. "Come on in."

"Well, I've got Flash. I was walking him. Would you like to sit out on the porch?"

Flo grabs a sweater from the coat tree stationed by the door and they sit down in the rocking chairs. Flash lies down on the rag rug.

"Seems like he's pretty used to that leash now," Flo says, and Teresa says, "You should have seen him five minutes ago. Pulling at the leash like a whirling dervish. But I won." She sighs.

Flo waits a beat, then asks, "You okay?"

"I'm sorry."

"What are you sorry for?"

"For . . ." She laughs. "I don't know."

"You can talk about anything you want with me, Teresa."

"Thank you."

"Can I talk about anything *I* want to?" Flo asks.

"Of course."

"All right. Let's us talk about love."

"Oh, jeez," Teresa says. "That again. All right, let's talk about it. Let me ask you, what exactly do you mean by 'love'?"

"Oh, you know, you meet someone—"

"There's a lot of different kinds of love," Teresa says. "For animals. For art. For travel. For solitude. For reading. For fudge."

Flo says, "I think you know I'm talking about people love. Loving a person. And them loving you back."

"Well, I love my clients. And they love me back. And it's a *safe* love."

"All right, Teresa, I'm just going to tell you right out. When I look at you, I see a beautiful soul, and a lonely one."

"I'm not lonely!"

"Well, all right," Flo says, "then I see a beautiful soul all by herself."

"It's okay to be by yourself."

"Not if you feel lonely. That's a sign that you want to be with someone. Now, tell me true, Teresa, wouldn't you like to be with someone in an intimate way? Just you and him? And I'm not talking about sex, I mean someone to talk to about things, someone to share things with, who will take care of you, who—"

"I know what you mean, Flo. Thank you. But it just doesn't seem to be in the cards for me to have that kind of relationship."

"Well, you know what? I did some research on dating sites."

Teresa looks over at her sharply.

"Over at the library," Flo says. "I went there, and I learned about all kinds of services for dating. And guess what. The librarian, her name is Mimi, she is also in her fifties, and she went on one of those sites, and she said it is definitely *not* too late for a fifty-something woman to find someone. It's not too late even for people much older than that."

Teresa says nothing, and Flo makes herself not push.

"And did *she* find someone?" Teresa finally asks.

"Well, not yet, but she had the gumption to try it, and she's still trying."

"Uh-huh."

"You do know, Teresa, that some people get married from those sites."

"So I've heard." Teresa shifts in her chair, looks at her watch, and starts to pick up Flash.

"All right," Flo says. "Let's change the subject. And let's us have some lemonade."

Teresa hands the leash to Flo. "Now you're talking. I'll go and get it. I know where it is."

When Teresa goes into the house, Flo pats her lap and the cat jumps into it. Flo speaks quietly into one pointed ear. "Work on her a little, will you?" She rocks a bit more and thinks of a friend who met up again with an old flame, just out of curiosity. They had been a hot item in their twenties; now they were in their seventies. They had lunch together and they had a nice time, though both of them had gone a little deaf and it was hard to hear each other. But they had a nice time, and the friend told Flo that when they parted, they embraced, and she whispered into his ear, "We ain't done with each other yet," and he whispered back in a way that she described as fierce, "I know we ain't." She won't tell Teresa that story. She won't talk any more about that kind of thing. Not today. But, oh, what makes a person so shy as to not take something off the platter that life passes around to them?

Teresa bangs out onto the porch and offers Flo a glass of lemonade. She must see something in Flo's face, because she smiles and says, "What."

Flo looks up and shrugs. "Nothing. I am just an old woman wearing my Keds with red socks and an apron over my housedress and I am looking out onto this evening and my heart is full."

Teresa leans over to put her hand over Flo's. "I like you so, so much."

"Ditto," Flo says. "Who wouldn't like you? Nobody, that's who."

A week later, when Teresa stops by, Flo says, "Teresa, I want to thank you for coming over here so often to visit with me."

"I like talking with you. You know that."

"But you're checking up on me, too, aren't you? I feel like I ought to pay you, Teresa. Can we agree upon a sum?"

"Flo. Please don't insult me that way."

"I didn't mean to insult you! It just seems that I'm taking up your time same as your other clients but I'm not giving you enough in return."

"Oh, Flo, you're giving me so much in return. Your friendship, for one."

All the friends Flo used to have are dead; she's the last one standing, something she never would have predicted. Yet here again is a friend. Well, life keeps on being life, unendingly surprising.

"And because of you, Flo, I've made a new friend, too."

Finally! Flo thinks. *A man!*

"Who?" Flo asks, trying unsuccessfully to sound casual.

"Mimi. The woman you met at the library. I went over and introduced myself, and we went out for lunch and talked about how if we were being honest, we didn't think a dating site would ever work for either of us, ever. But we sure did like each other."

"I guess I won't get hired to be the host of *The Dating Game*."

"Well, you'll like this. I did go out on a date just yesterday. Just for coffee."

"Isn't that wonderful! Who is he? Where did you meet him?"

"I've known him for a while. He's a cashier at the grocery store I go to." She smiles. "He's funny. And just . . . *nice*. We talk a lot whenever he rings me up; I always go to his line. So the other day he asked if we could have coffee. And we did."

"Can you give me some juicy details?" Flo asks.

"Not really," Teresa says, and she is staring hard into her lap.

"Well, you two take all the time you need. Seems to me the best relationships come when you can take your time. You just go at your own pace. Sooner or later, I hope you'll—"

"Let's not get ahead of ourselves," Teresa says. "I don't think we'll really work out or anything."

"You didn't like him?"

"No, I liked him a lot. He has a parakeet named Zelda that he lets fly around his house. He said the bird knows where the crackers are and she always flies to that cupboard when she wants one. He cooks at a soup kitchen every Saturday. He just bought an electric bike, and he said he saved up for it in a Mason jar just like when he was a kid and saved up for his first Schwinn. Said he eschewed the bell this time, but he might get streamers. But . . . things just don't last for me, Flo. Sometimes it's them, more often it's me. I just end up . . . I just stop."

"*Why?*"

"I guess I get disappointed. I end up thinking it's better for me to be alone."

Flo gets tight in the chest like she might even cry and says, "Oh, Teresa. Hasn't your work taught you how very little time any of us has? And how much richer life is when—"

"My life *is* rich, Flo. Honestly! My work, my hobbies. My freedom! It seems that people never believe you can be fine alone, but you *can* be. Whenever I try to have a relationship, I find I have too many unrealistic expectations."

"Like what?"

Teresa leans her head back onto the rocker and closes her eyes. "I ought to write scripts for Disney. I always want something *wonderful* to happen."

"Such as?"

"Oh, I don't know."

"Sure you do. Yank out something deep in your heart that you wish he would do, and tell me what it is."

"Okay. Well, I guess what I would love is if he would call me late at night and say 'Don't get dressed, just get ready for me to come by and pick you up in fifteen minutes.' And then he would drive me out of town in my nightie and make me get out of his car and tell me to look at the stars and the immense black sky and then he would say, 'I need all this room to hold the feelings I have for you. And have had, for a long time.'"

Teresa has been talking like she was in a dream, but now she seems to snap back into herself. "Good grief, I guess I'm under the influence of your romantic ways. What a dumb idea."

"It's not a dumb idea. I suggest *you* do it to *him*!"

Teresa points to herself and raises her eyebrows.

"Why not?" Flo asks. "Not everyone seems to know this but a lot of men like romantic things just as much as women do."

"Huh."

"They do!"

"Oh, all right, maybe I will."

"Say you will for sure. Tonight!"

"But we're going out again tonight. For Italian food."

"All the better," Flo says. "Do it tonight. After he drops you off at home, wait an hour and then call him and say what you told me. He will like it, I promise you. Who doesn't like a romantic adventure? Don't think beyond it, don't think what it means or will mean, just do it because it's fun. And then tell me what happens tomorrow, will you do that?" Flo's heart has begun beating like a jackrabbit's. She'd better calm down. She'd better *lie* down. She leans forward and touches Teresa's hand. It's such a small hand. She says, "Now look, Teresa, I hate to play this card, but it might be an old lady's last wish." She starts coughing, as fake as can be, and Teresa laughs.

"I *would* look upon it as a favor," Flo says, and Teresa says, "Oh, all right, I'll do it, but I'm only going to show him the stars and not say anything else; those words I imagined him saying, that was just a flight of fancy. It's way too soon to think either one of us is anywhere near to saying such a thing."

"Oh?" Flo says. "Are you sure about that?"

"I'll do what I said," Teresa says, and Flo knows she will do it, too. She's one of those who if she says she'll do it, no matter what it is, she'll do it. There aren't a lot of people like that. And she doesn't have to say any romantic words when she takes that fellow out into the night. The stars will talk for her.

After Flo comes into the house, she rests on the sofa before she goes upstairs. Satisfaction lies within her like a curled-up cat, but Lordy, she's tired. She closes her eyes and thinks about Teresa and the cashier. She hopes Teresa stops being so scared; that's all it is, she is plum scared to risk having certain feelings. But Flo hopes Teresa can tell that new man a tender thought or two and that he'll hold them like he would a newborn.

You know, Ruthie, there are times in a woman's life when she looks at her frying pan sideways with her arms crossed. Sometimes when that feeling came over me Terrence and I would go out, maybe he would even just take us over to McDonald's, and it always felt like a treat. I never was one for: It has to be white tablecloths and a straight-backed waiter reciting the specials like highfalutin poetry. No, I got right nervous in such places all my life and not because I came up poor. It was something else, like people all pretending something and I did not want to pretend along with them. For shame, Flo, Terrence used to say. These people are just coming out to eat and the restaurant is trying to make it special. There's nothing wrong with that. I would tell him he was right because he was. But a person just can't help having those chafey feelings sometimes.

I have been doing so well lately I wonder if I will live a lot longer than that doctor thought. But I am leaving this letter which I now call War and Peace on the kitchen table just in case. I reckon I could have just called you and told you I'm leaving you my house and all my things. But I'm aiming for a surprise. I don't know why. Well, maybe I do. Who doesn't like surprises when it means you're getting something interesting from someone who loves you.

I want to tell you about the rubber band I mentioned a while back, what it means to me and why I kept it. It's in the top left kitchen drawer in a little white box with a red ribbon tied around it, you'll find it. Now, I have advertised this like it was the Second Coming and I hope you won't be disappointed with the story. I hope you won't stand with one hand on your hip saying well for Pete's sake.

Here goes.

One time Terrence and I were in a contemplative mood, sitting at the kitchen table. I was right where I am now and Terrence was sitting where there is an empty chair, always an empty chair now, though I am not shy to say I do see him there sometimes, his shirt open at the collar and his sleeves rolled up and his beautiful big hands clasped together. Sitting there smiling at me. Sometimes he is see-through and sometimes he is not. Sometimes he's just so real. And at those times I can near about smell his aftershave, I believe he's calling me to him.

But the rubber band. Terrence and I were newly married, he had just come back from the war, and I had caught a case of the insecures. I kept thinking terrible thoughts like what if his love dies, what if we get in such a terrible fight there is no repairing it and we go down in bitterness. I loved him then in a kind of desperate way. I felt like I needed to walk behind him with my hand on his belt lest he get away. He was my most precious thing, and I was scared to death he'd leave again and I'd lose him. I couldn't talk to Terrence about this; I didn't know where these feelings were coming from, although later, I saw that somehow I must have known something.

One Sunday afternoon we'd just come back from church, and we were having a cup of coffee at this kitchen table and I busted out crying. Why sweetheart, what is wrong? he asked. I didn't answer and he came around to my side of the table and got on his knees like he was proposing (like he was supposed to do the first time around). I commenced to blubbering harder. And bless his heart he just stayed quiet and kneeling even though I'd plum forgot to sweep the kitchen floor the night before. Finally, I managed to tell him a bit of what was in my heart, that we might come apart somehow. Hm, he said, and he got up and he went into the drawer where we kept our rubber bands. He pulled one out and brought it to the table and laid it before me and my splotchy face. See this? he asked, pointing to it. Yes, I said. Watch, he said, and he pulled that rubber band out so far his hands were trembling and I feared it would bust. See that? he said, and I said yes. Then he lowered that stretched-out rubber band to the floor and let it go. And of course it snapped right back into place. Terrence picked it up and held it in his hand before me. What do you see now? he asked. I said I saw a rubber band. But what has happened to it? he asked like he was Mr. Wizard. I said, Well, it has gone back to its shape. Right, he said, and that is what we will always do. You can never do anything that will undo my love for you. We will have fights, and I suspect we might call each other names and maybe sometimes we will have private regrets. But always we will come back to our original shape, which is that I love you. Period. Always we will come back to that. I know it and I think you know it too. Let us accept that there will be problems but never mind, human minds and hearts and souls are resilient. He looked at his watch and he said, And now I suggest we stop talking about all this doom and gloom and get on over to Miss Lee's Café before they run out of meatloaf.

I'll be ready in just a minute, I said. I spect he figured I had to piddle or was putting on my lipstick, in those days you didn't hardly take out the trash without wearing lipstick. And I did put on some lipstick in a lovely red shade but then I did what I really wanted which was to put that rubber band Terrence had used for his demonstration into a little white box. I put it in there like its own little house and then I tied a red ribbon on it. And when times of trouble came between us all I had to do was look at that box and trust would come again to my heart. You'll see the box there, Ruthie. I can't hardly think it will be worth keeping. But the story might tie itself up in red ribbon and live on in you.

That Terrence. I'll tell you, his love was light as a feather and heavy as an anvil both at the same time, love can be like that, and my dear dear Ruthie I hope it was like that for you and Jonathan and if it was I truly believe you can find it again. Things change shape, and then they can go back. They can.

"Oh, hell's bells," Flo mutters, sitting up at the side of her bed. It's 4:50 A.M. and it's been a restless night, her tossing and turning from side to side and lying wide-eyed on her back all exasperated and staring up at the ceiling as though she were begging it to help her.

She turns on the nightstand lamp, slides into her slippers, and creeps quietly down into the kitchen, though why she is being so quiet she has no idea. She could do the Tarzan yell and nobody would know. But it's habit, to be quiet getting up in the night. Same as she still sleeps on her side of the bed, and the same as she sometimes reaches over as if Terrence might be there. One time she really thought he *was* there, but it was just how longing can take a shape sometimes.

She pulls on a cardigan she left on the back of a kitchen chair. It's an old gray one with leather buttons that belonged to her father, and she wonders if she should tell Ruthie about it—how whenever she puts it on she sees him beckoning to her to come sit on his lap and listen to the ballgame on the radio with him. Maybe not. There's so much else to tell her about, and Flo is beginning to feel that she'd better get moving and finish this letter. For one quick second, she wonders if this whole enterprise isn't futile, if all it will do is make Ruthie feel tired and overburdened. But then she is right back to believing she should do it—she *must* do it. Not only for Ruthie, but for herself. An autobiography in *things*, that's what this letter is.

She starts to turn on the overhead, but her spirit is feeling too delicate for an overhead just yet. Instead, she makes coffee by the light of the moon.

She sits at the table with her hands folded as the coffee finishes perking, then pours some into her Mrs. Hen mug and goes out to sit on the front porch to watch the day crack open. She once had a friend say that nothing good happens after dark. "Nothing??" Flo had asked, teasing her; they were young then, and rambunctious with their husbands at night. The friend—Connie was her name—waved her hand, and then she leaned forward and said something Flo has never forgotten. She said, "I'm just talking about all the good stuff that happens in the day, the *life* all around you: bumblebees, and children off to school and people working at all kinds of things. People going and coming, all day long, and I always wonder what all they're *do*ing." She looked at Flo then, with a kind of shyness Flo had not seen in her before, and she asked, "Do you do that, Flo, do you watch people like that?" Flo said, "I am too busy working to do that." And then Connie kind of tucked herself back in and Flo felt ashamed. People, when they tell you certain things, they want you to agree. They want you at least to see what they mean, in your heart. That was a time she had failed a friend.

Flo watches the sky turn pink, then apricot, then yellow, and finally blue. She watches as the papers get flung onto porches and she listens to the sleepy birds commence their daily symphony. She sees a man carrying a briefcase going out to his car: there is the muted thunk of the door closing, the stuttering sound of the engine starting, and the whine of reverse. Whoever the man is drives past Flo and waves hello, and she waves back. Terrence told her once about a language where there is no word for "hello." Rather, people greet each other by saying, "You are here." And the response is "Yes, I am." And in another language Flo had heard about—in Africa, she thinks—people don't say, on parting, "I'll see you." They say, "Somehow."

Flo doesn't know why remembering this now brings tears to her eyes. Well, yes, she does. *Somehow* is a wish made without being able to know whether or not it can come true. It is determination in the face of uncertainty.

Down the block, a light goes on upstairs, then downstairs. Flo sips at her coffee and she thinks, I ought to have followed the sun all my life: wake up when it rises, lie down when it sets. It seems like such a good idea now, if not exactly practical. Or doable, really. It's just wishful thinking, an idea come too late. Or an idea like people get all the time, ideas that do not come to fruition because people mostly return to their habits, good or bad. But this day of noticing? This is for Connie. Rest her soul.

Ruthie, I want to thank you for giving me a job, that being all I'm telling you about my life. I have enjoyed telling you about certain things but mostly I have enjoyed revisiting memories like I'm watching home movies again, the film whirring along, the images shown on a sheet hung up in a darkened living room. I hadn't counted on remembering all these things, but I'm glad I did.

I realize I'm leaving you a lot to read through and I hope you won't be mad. I don't think you will. I do hope you're able to use some of my things, maybe something that will make you remember being a little girl becoming good friends with your neighbor, Flo. I believe you were eight years old when you asked if I wanted to be blood sisters with you, and didn't we prick our fingers and do it.

I just got a picture in my head of your being here in this house after I'm gone, wearing nice slacks and a pretty blouse and your hair in a ponytail. A somber expression as you go rooting through the drawers, and maybe you'll be a little flustered, but tell you what, you just quick take what you want and then call those fellers who take away junk. Then you can sell the house and that will be fine. I won't know WHAT you do so don't you worry about me. I won't know what you do unless there's an afterlife where I would be like an angel floating above you, and if I were an angel I sure wouldn't be making judgments or getting fussy about what you do with my house. No, I think I would have a pulled-back kind of mind at that point.

But look at me wandering off as usual. Let us get down to business.

You once were playing Rich Lady and I made you some lemonade and put it in one of those beautiful crystal glasses that are in a box in the basement. Seems like nobody wants such things anymore, problems with where to store them, and they seem fussy, I suppose. But I hope you'll just look at the etchings on them again, and see how pretty they are. You seemed to like it when we used one that day. And I remember I cut crusts off your peanut butter sandwich, and you sat straight as a board wearing your tutu and a striped t-shirt that you'd slid off your shoulders to be your strapless gown. You had a pair of my high heels over your socks, and you had on my jewelry, too, all you could fit on yourself. I remember you had on my blue rhinestone earrings and that wasn't enough so you clipped the red and white polka dot earrings onto your glasses. You were done up and I took a picture of you I still have, you might find it in one of my albums and offer it to your children. Oh, what children's joyful freedom can do for us, seems like a parched lawn being watered, being around them sometimes. And you in particular, Miss Ruthie, you always had something going, I didn't ever know what you would have in your wagon, one time you were peddling rocks and you sure enough sold some, some were agates and right pretty. I myself bought one for thirty cents and it's still in my nightstand drawer. You'll find it.

I spent a lot of time with you when you were a girl. And a fair amount when you got to the terrible teens and didn't hardly want to spend time with anyone, including yourself, it seemed. Even so, you would come to sit with me, and we would pass the time. You with your sparkle fingernail polish, perfectly applied, not all messy like when you were little. I would look over at you and think, She's going to be a beautiful woman. And I would think, If she were mine, I would have named her Glory. I didn't tell you that, although now I think maybe you would have liked to hear it. My, what we don't say in our lifetimes. But there I go a-wandering again.

I got some old suits from the 1940s good as new. I've heard some young people like the vintage look so there you go. I got an old telephone in the basement makes a *click-click-click* sound when the rotary dial spins back from dialing, I wonder would your kids like that. I have a copy of that book *Gone With the Wind* someone told me was worth money what with the way the author signed her name in it. I have tablecloths from the '30s with nary a stain, they might work fine for a picnic. I don't know of a much better thing than a perfect day and a hamper and a tree generous with shade. And of course your sweetheart there to share it all, sitting cross-legged on the blanket. I haven't sat cross-legged for years, and I'm tempted to try it now but I know I can't do it so why remind myself. Anyway, I might get stuck and no one here to unstick me.

I have some fountain pens that are true works of art, and I have some turquoise ink left, that was always my favorite. I have plenty of greeting cards in a drawer in the basement, right down there in the laundry room cupboard, some are real old but I believe there is a market for them or maybe your friends would like to receive them. Nobody gets much mail anymore and a pretty Valentine from long ago might soften someone's hard day, you never know. Oh and embroidered dishcloths and pillowcases and some picture frames might as well be reused. Some useful things, Ruthie. To me they are so useful.

Flo startles awake from where she has been resting on the sofa. Her breathing has gone all raggedy, and there's a sharp pain in her back. This must be it. Is it *it*? She straightens her legs and arranges her hands over her chest but then that bothers her, how it's like in a coffin, so she lets her arms rest plain at her sides. There is her watch on her wrist, ticking away. Here she is on the precipice, she thinks she's on the precipice, ready for Judgment Day.

Outside, a horn honks. It's like that Emily Dickinson poem she read in high school where the person is dying and she hears a fly buzz. Flo always thought that was a strange poem. But here she is, and she hears a horn honk, and it's different now.

Judgment Day. Whenever Flo used to think of that, she always imagined God on a high stool at a high desk peering down over His bifocals. How many people did He see? So many people dying all the time, seems like the line would be awful long. Some people think God is very human, and if He is He would sure enough get a sore fanny sitting there that long. And the poor human being trembling before Him, wondering, *What will the verdict be?* If God really is human, wouldn't He be able to see what makes a person do whatever they did and have mercy? What does make one person good and another person bad? Surely they're not born that way. She thinks of a new life blinking in the light and some voice saying to that baby, still blue in its hands, "Now, you. You'll be a murderer." No. Surely it doesn't work that way. Some unfortunate souls get poor soil and poor water. Course there's the ones get poor soil and water and yet still they thrive, like those flowers grow up in the cracks in the sidewalk. Wouldn't God know everything? Wouldn't He take everything into account? And if He did, wouldn't everyone go to heaven? Flo expects there's room. For heaven's sake, there's George Washington up there with his wooden teeth and all, all, all the ones before him. And pets, it would be nice if—

Suddenly, her breathing goes regular and slow. There is no pain. She opens her eyes and crosses her ankles, waits for a moment, then sits up. Smooths down her hair in the back. Here she still is. *You are here.* She has to stop wasting time and finish that letter.

She goes into the kitchen and sits down at the table. That had been something, to think that she was going. She had not been afraid. She had been something else. Not comforted, but something close to that. Eased. Lifted. She remembers hearing about that one famous actress who was dying and she got up in the night and her husband came out and put his arms around her and she began to weep, saying, "I want to go home." And he said you are home. "No," she said. "I want to go home."

Flo believes she understands her now.

But she is still in *this* home, and after she works on her letter she is going to call Teresa and see can she come for lunch. "Pick up your favorite takeout," she'll tell her. "My treat." Flo's got fifty bucks in her purse, easy.

I got some things you might overlook that could prove useful to you. I keep clothespins in a cloth bag in the laundry room. Now, you might not want to use them for hanging wash, but they are good for other things, too. I clothespin letters together that I walk to the mailbox. They work just fine for closing up bags of chips and cookies. I even use them for bookmarks in my magazines. And you stuck some in the dirt one time to make a corral for your plastic horses, didn't you love your palomino.

I guess this is probably a foolish thing to tell you about. But I'm not going to cross it all out and have you wonder what I had said. You'd probably think it was something real exciting or embarrassing when it is just me saying how much I like clothespins. I feel that way about buttons, too. These odd little loves that we have and seldom tell other people about. And yet in some ways don't they make the world go round.

Flo is sitting on the front porch waiting to have lunch with Teresa, who just called to say she'd be ten minutes late; the line at Uggabooga's had been long. Teresa said she had gotten Thanksgiving sandwiches; she hoped that was okay. "Those are my favorite," Flo had told her, just as she'd told Teresa that Uggabooga's was her favorite restaurant. It got its name from the owner, whose nickname came from the time he was just a little toddler and his parents called him that just to make him laugh. Next thing you know his friends called him that, all the way up to college. His wife calls him Boog.

Across the street, in the house where two little girls live, Flo sees the front porch screen door bang open, and the smaller girl, who is maybe five years old, comes stomping out with a roller bag made for kids: a teddy bear on wheels with a zipper in his belly. "And I am *never* coming *back*!" the girl says, over her shoulder. "I *hate* you!"

The girl bumps her suitcase down the steps, then sits on the bottom one, thinking. She looks up the street, then down. She scratches her arm, inspecting the sky, where storm clouds have lowered, and now here comes a long and low rumble of thunder, sounding almost like a dog's growl. The girl rises and walks slowly to the end of the walkway, then turns around and goes back inside. Quickly.

Well, then.

Flo imagines the girl standing in the hallway, defeated, her mother coming down the stairs. She hopes for forgiveness all around.

When Flo was a little girl, she was very taken with her next-door neighbors, who were childless, and who always had time for Flo. They liked to teach Flo things. The woman taught Flo how to whisk egg whites into meringue, and how to crank the handle of the ice cream maker. The husband taught her how to read baseball scores in the newspaper and how to pitch a horseshoe. Flo could come over to their house whenever she wanted, and she didn't even have to knock. She used to sit in the parlor, straight-backed in a big horsehair chair, and regard the light coming through the lace curtains. She would pretend she was someone very important who had stopped by to visit, and in her experience important people shared interesting news of one kind or another. One time she told them, "I ate some dog biscuits today."

"What did you do *that* for?" the Mrs. asked.

Flo said, "I just wanted to taste them and also I was playing dog."

"Well, that sounds perfectly reasonable," the Mr. said.

Such an old, old memory, but Flo can feel again the rough texture of the chair beneath her, and she remembers how that room always smelled like toast to her. She supposed she was to those neighbors what Ruthie was to her, a pretend daughter, a nice fill-in for a wide hurt.

When Flo decided to run away, at age seven, she'd wanted to find a family like that one to live with all the time. It couldn't be her next-door neighbors; she had to be farther away than that so her parents could never find her. She used a shoebox for a suitcase and put in a pair of underwear, a nightgown, her toothbrush and hairbrush, and some caramels twisted up in wax paper. Her book of fairy tales wouldn't fit, so she carried it separately. She went out into the field behind her house and found a big rock and sat on it to consider things. A horny toad sat motionless, having a beady-eyed look at her, and she thought about trying to catch him. She liked to look at horny toads close up; they reminded her of when dinosaurs roamed, and she liked too the way their necks looked like old men's necks, all stretched and tough and wrinkly. But she didn't try to catch him. She stared at her feet for a while and then she got up and went home.

Here comes Teresa, pulling up to the curb. Flo can hardly wait to dig into *her.* Why, it's been like a good old-fashioned soap opera, seeing what has happened with Teresa and speculating about what *might* happen. Flo thinks that being curious about things is one of the pulls that makes people want to keep on moving forward, and she's grateful to Teresa for her very own *Days of Our Lives.*

I'll tell you true, Ruthie, this is a crowded house. Long about in my mid-seventies, I saw it was happening that my things were beginning to own me rather than the other way around. So many things! Seems like a lot of people begin at some point to get concerned about that, mostly women, as they are the more responsible of the species, let's put the cards on the table, it's usually the women doing most of the organizing and caretaking and the decision-making. Lord, sometimes it seemed like men belonged to a cub scout troop where we women were ever the den mothers.

But this sorting-out business. It didn't seem like any of us ever got too far, seemed like almost always things simply got left to the children. I once thought, I'm going to hire someone to help me and she doesn't even have to help me. She can just stand by me and make some nice comments on things every now and then and encourage me to toss the things I just don't need anymore nor have I needed them for a long time. But what if my imaginary helper and I agreed that I do NOT need these skeins of yarn I've had for nigh onto sixty years and then it turns out you would have loved them?

I had another idea once for getting rid of things, which was to put a table out on my sidewalk with a sign: FREE IF YOU LOVE IT AND WILL TAKE CARE OF IT. Like everything on the table was a kitten when in fact it might be a screen to prevent splatters when you fry things, or a half-slip I never did wear, or a pencil sharpener, who can't use a pencil sharpener if they don't have one? I like the old-fashioned wall-mounted kind we used to have in school. I got to be the pencil-sharpener emptier and I looked upon it as quite an honor. Each day I would march to the trash can by the teacher's desk and empty that pencil sharpener of its fragrant shavings, they smelled like lead and cedar and to this day I love that smell.

So many things. I got some love letters in a cardboard box from Terrence. We always agreed, Terrence and I, that whoever outlasted the other would destroy those letters. I guess we thought we might be embarrassed by the content but let me tell you something, we were embarrassed by things like this: "I not only love you, I need you." Now what is embarrassing about that when nowadays people get on those computers and you can see them stark naked. And you don't even know them, nor they you, they are just parading around naked, Look at me, look at me. I heard they show everything and sometimes they do a lot more than just parade around. I don't like to think of people doing that. I guess I'm more modest than that. I used to fuss if my bra strap showed and whoever I was with didn't tell me. Same as food on your face, you know, you might be embarrassed if someone tells you that you got a big blob of mayonnaise at the corner of your mouth, but then you are grateful no one else will see it. I used to know a man a few years back, he was even older than I, and he wore his t-shirts inside out. I one time said, Say did you know your t-shirt is inside out? I said it soft, I didn't want to embarrass him. He said yes he did know. Oh, I said, and I pondered his flat response. Then I said, Why? He said I don't like seams. I said, Well, you know people might think you wore it inside out by accident, and he stopped walking and turned to look me full in the face to say, I never did care about WHAT people thought of me. I never did feel like I owed all these EXPLANATIONS other people feel they need to offer all the time. Well, you are free, then, I said, with a little spark of admiration, and he said, Yes I am. And listen to this, Ruthie, didn't I see some teenaged boys a few days later got THEIR t-shirts turned inside out like it was a fashion statement, which I guess to them it was. Oh, those boys were riding along fast down the middle of the street, and one would commence to punch another one, and soon they were all punching and laughing, seemed like their heads were full of fun. And I'll bet they were thinking they would live forever, don't we all think that. Why, I'm almost thinking that now, even, that even though death sure enough has his Florence Greene assignment, he will pass me by and I will have some more time for my new friends and for me and Champ just setting out on the porch, I do love that dog.

I might have had a dog after Terrence died. Although getting a dog in old age reminds me of my friend Mary Curtin who had to go to the hospital right quick with a heart attack. I got to see her just before she died and she was so concerned about her dog and who would feed him that night. I knew her dog, Woodson was his name, he was one of those black and white dogs had what looked like freckles on his nose and a saddle patch on his back. I said I would feed him and I would keep him too but I didn't. I found someone else to do it. I still feel bad about that, but I couldn't face what if I took him and then I had to leave him, too.

About a week after I brought him home, I was out walking him, and I passed by a young family the next block over. They were on their lawn, the children playing croquet, a lovely game you hardly ever see played anymore, but the children came up to admire him and I all of a sudden got an idea and I asked would they like to have him, he was old but he was right healthy, nothing wrong with him, and he ate just plain old regular dog food. Those children's eyes grew wide as hibiscus blossoms and they started yelling about how this lady is giving this dog away, can we have him, can we pleeeeeeease???? The parents came over and gave old Woodson the once-over and said, Well why not. I handed them the leash and I walked away. I did look back once and that dog had his back to me and was wagging his tail something fierce so I thought, Okay then. He will have a better home. I lied to my friend Mary Curtin, but he will have a better home. I got back to my house and picked up the dishes I had used to feed Woodson and I cleaned them out and I felt the little burn of tears that wanted to come but I would not let them. I kept thinking, He has a better home, and I knew it was true, yet my sorrow made me feel like something had come along and scooped something out of me. I guess it was that special love you can have for animals and I knew it wasn't coming back anytime soon and indeed it never did come back at all.

But I did keep Woodson's dishes. They are light blue bowls with white insides and they are way at the back of my bottom cupboard next to the stove. I didn't want to come across them but I just couldn't throw them away. However briefly, he'd been my dog.

Flo awakened in early morning, dressed, took a walk clean around the block, and felt strong as Spartacus. Hours later, she *still* feels strong as Spartacus, and she's dying to tell someone about the adventure she just had. Teresa is at work, though, and Flo is hard-pressed to think of someone else she might share this story with. But then she remembers Mildred.

She walks the short distance to Mildred's house and knocks on the door. It is opened immediately.

"Remember last time we visited, and you told me that story about ice skating?" Flo asks Mildred. "Now I got a story to share with you."

"Oh, goody," Mildred says, without a trace of irony. "Come on in."

When the women are seated at the kitchen table, Flo says, "Now. I took a walk today, just around the block. And you know that creek runs behind the Millers' house, the one with wildflowers growing up all alongside?"

"Yes, I love that creek. You can catch polliwogs there."

"You catch polliwogs?" Flo looks around the kitchen as though she might see a jar full of them bumping into each other.

Mildred laughs. "No, but the neighborhood kids do."

"Oh. Well, anyway, when I went by there, there was a man sitting down close to the water. There was a smell I noticed, and his clothes were none too clean. But he seemed peaceful, you know, butterflies flitting by him, and him not moving except to raise a sandwich to his mouth. I called out to him, 'Hello there!' He turned around quick and his face was full of worry; maybe he thought he was going to get kicked out of the neighborhood. But I waved and said again, 'Hello!' and then he smiled a most beautiful smile. Not many teeth, but a beautiful smile.

"I asked him was he having a picnic. 'Just eating a fried egg sandwich,' he said. I told him that was one of my favorites, and he said, 'Come and join me, we can share!'"

"Uh-oh," Mildred says.

"Now, I was afraid, too, Mildred, even though it was broad daylight, but I said to myself, Oh, what's the difference?" It occurs to Flo to tell Mildred about her diagnosis, but she doesn't want to, not yet. It will interrupt her story, which she is having a fine time telling. She says, "What I mean is, I thought, At my age I'm on my way out anyway, and if this man up and murders me I'll only be on my way a bit sooner."

Mildred frowns. "You didn't really think he would do *that,* did you?"

"I guess not. I guess we just get programmed to be afraid of certain things. Anyway, I asked the man, I said, 'Do you really have enough to share?' and he said all hearty, 'Of course I do!' Said, 'You can have this half, it's clean,' and he held it up wrapped in a napkin and his eyes were all squinched up friendly in the sunlight. I inched closer but I didn't get too far because the uneven ground was too hard for me. The man got up and came on over to me. He was tall and real skinny, with such gentleness in his eyes. He handed me the sandwich and I took a quick peek inside to make sure it looked safe. I suppose it was rude to do that, but I just felt I had to. Well, not only did it look all right, it smelled wonderful. 'Where did you buy this?' I asked him and he said, 'I didn't buy it, there's a lady who drops by food for me sometimes. Her name is Anne, she lives across the street. She's maybe in her eighties, but very strong. Do you know her?' I said I didn't think so. He said, 'She wears a little top-knot? And she has bangs and very intense eyes that seem to almost burn into you?' I said no, I didn't know her. 'Well, I guess she likes to feed people,' he said.

"He patted his breast pocket and pulled out a pack of cigarettes, all bent and battered. He asked did I want one and I said no thank you and he looked at the pack and put it back in his pocket. '*You* can smoke,' I said, and he said, 'Nah, it's a filthy habit. I just can't quit it altogether.' He said, 'I started when I was nine years old.' 'Nine years old!' I said, and he just shrugged. He asked me, 'Don't you have any bad habits that started in childhood?' I said most likely, but I couldn't think of any now. He said, 'You'll think of some later. Most likely when you're trying to go to sleep tonight.'

"I took a bite of the sandwich he'd given me and it was a lovely mix of warm fried egg and salt and pepper and butter. My appreciation must have shown on my face because the man said, 'Yeah, that's one of my favorites that she gives me.' He told me his name was Archie and I told him my name. He said, 'Are you Flo all the time?' I said, 'Well, yes, that's my *name*.' He said, 'I like to change my name every day. Today I'm Archie.'

"'What were you yesterday?' I asked. He thought for a minute and then he said, 'Oh yeah. Floyd.'

"I told him I used to have a milkman named Floyd and I sure did like him and his cheerful demeanor, always smiling, Floyd was. He had a gold tooth seemed to flash out Good morning! Good morning! I said, 'That's a good name, Floyd.'

"'Not as good as Archie,' he said, and I just nodded. I won't say I agreed with him, but there was no use in souring the moment with a petty disagreement."

"Too soon for a first fight," Mildred says.

"Right. But I thought Archie had a good idea with a different name for every day, and I told him if I had a name for me today it would be Maria. 'No,' he said. 'What do you mean, *no*?' I asked, and he said, 'That name doesn't suit you.' 'What name does?' I asked him, and he said, 'Julia.'

"'Julia!' I said. And I was pleased because I thought Julia was a right pretty name."

"It is a pretty name," Mildred says. "And it does suit you."

Flo has an urge to look into a mirror as if to confirm that, but there is the story to finish.

"I asked Archie, 'Where does this Anne person live?' 'Over yonder,' he said, and he pointed to a little white house with a picket fence around it, something you might see in a children's book. I asked Archie if he would introduce me to Anne. He told me to just knock at her door, she was real nice. As for him, he had to go and meet up with some pals in town. 'Gotta go to Bum Club,' he said, and laughed this real raspy laugh.

"I started toward Anne's house but then I turned back."

"Why?" Mildred asks.

"Two reasons. One is I thought maybe I'd like to find her a little gift because of how she gifted others. The other reason is I thought maybe I would hold that idea inside to look forward to. I'm sure you've heard this, Mildred, but they say you need someone to love, something to do—"

"And something to look forward to," Mildred says.

"Right. So that is one of my something to look forward tos. I want to write a little note thanking Anne for her regular kindnesses. You remember how Lady Bird Johnson had flowers planted all along the highway? That's how I feel about these things. One person does one nice thing, and it blooms in the breast of another. Pass it on. Sometimes the strife in this world makes me think I must be silly to have such hope for the spread of good. But I have it anyway. You never know when something is going to hike your spirit up. Like when that man told me something as he was leaving; he looked back over his shoulder and he said, 'I never did know what kindness was in the world until I admitted my need for it.'"

Mildred sits back in her chair. "Flo, would you give me permission to write an article about this? Would that be okay?"

"Well, of course it would!"

"I think if a magazine takes it, it might make a nice Christmas story. I'll have it framed for you."

". . . Oh," Flo says, and Mildred says, "What's wrong?" and so Flo tells her she won't be around at Christmas, and why. And here's what Mildred does: she puts her hand over

Flo's and looks clear and direct at her. And that is all and that is everything: a friend talking to a friend and the sun coming through the kitchen window and the birds yakking in the backyard trees and the way Flo might be gone but the story will be there.

Today I found Terrence's collection of pocket watches and I hope you'll be thrilled when you see them. They are something to behold, all engraved and many of the faces illustrated with flowers and birds, and the second hands so delicate you wonder that they didn't disintegrate into thin air years ago. Terrence got those watches from his grandfather and he cherished them so much he never would use them. He liked to just sit in his chair of a Sunday afternoon and look at them and reminisce. His grandfather was not an affectionate person, but he knew Terrence liked those pocket watches, and when Terrence was a little boy, his grandfather would pull him onto his lap and let him touch them. It was the only time he ever let Terrence get close to him, and so I expect the watches were imbued with something more than beauty. Terrence had a soft cloth he would polish the watches with after he looked at them, and then he would put them away. I found them in a box on the top shelf of his closet, I had completely overlooked them for all these years. And now they are yours.

Four in the afternoon. This is the time of day I used to start dinner preparations. I'm not cooking much these days but I still have my metal box full of recipes and you might like some of them. Remember when you first tasted my hamburger stroganoff? You were loath to try it because you said it looked like dog throw-up. But then you did try it and commenced to eat practically the whole thing. It's in the recipe box that I'll leave out on the counter by the sink.

In the basement, on a train table, is Terrence's set-up for his model trains. He was embarrassed by how much he loved those trains and by how he loved to play with them. But I thought it was wonderful. One year I got him an engineer's cap for Christmas, and he wore it, too. Sometimes I'd be upstairs and I'd hear him tooting that train's whistle downstairs and it never failed to make me smile. We'd always wanted to take a train trip clear across the country, Terrence and I, but we never did. I don't rightly know why. But I'd hear that whistle blow and I'd imagine us sleeping at night in the little beds, one above the other, the velvet curtains pulled, and the landscape whooshing by. I liked to think of it snowing hard outside, and us lying there and peeking out our windows, no worries about having to drive through a storm.

If you ask me, toy trains are always special, but Terrence's were nigh onto exquisite, the little coal car complete with pellets to make it really smoke. Scenery all around, people and little stores and even a black cocker spaniel on a red leash. Now I have to tell you a sad thing, which is that these trains were meant to go to a little boy used to come and watch Terrence play with the trains, and Terrence let him blow the whistle, and sometimes he let the boy drive the train too, but the boy had a tendency to go too fast around the curves and derail. Terrence would get kind of mad when that happened and one day he yelled at the boy, who was eight years old, he yelled that if he was really driving that train he would have maybe killed some people by derailing. Well, the boy commenced to crying and he ran out of the house, and there I was standing in the kitchen with my laundry basket at my hip thinking, What happened? What's wrong? And there on the table were the snickerdoodles I'd set out for him and Terrence just sitting there, glasses of milk to go along. After I watched the boy go tearing down the block, still crying, Terrence came walking up slow and shame-faced from the basement and sat at the kitchen table and I asked him what had happened. He didn't answer for a long time and then he was very soft-spoken, telling me, and he wondered why he'd been so mean. I still had never talked to Terrence about what happened in the War, and I thought maybe the notion of killing people was what had gotten Terrence so upset. I was fixing to gently ask him, but then Terrence said it was likely that the boy, Robin was his name, Robin Miller, he'd likely not ever come back because he was a very sensitive boy. Now I'll always be that mean man to him, Terrence said, and he commenced to rub one hand with the other. I went to kneel before him and I took his hands into my own. It was a mistake, I told him. We all make mistakes. But that didn't seem to help. Terrence said, That boy will never come back, and I wish I could just give him the trains, but I don't think he'd take them now. I said, In time he will come back, as though I knew for sure, and you know I did feel sure. But it seemed the boy never did recover or else he went on to other things. I don't believe Terrence ever got over that, and he said maybe it was good he and I never had children since look how delicate everything could be. You have Ruthie, Terrence said, but I have lost my Robin. I didn't know what to say then. I just sat with him and eventually he bit into a cookie and I got up and sat across from him and I had one, too.

I would like you to give those trains to some boy would appreciate them if you can, Ruthie. No money exchanged. Just give them to a boy whose eyes will light up at the opportunity. Now be sure to tell him to wear that engineer's cap.

Flo is in her nightgown making coffee when her phone rings. When she answers, she hears, "I did it!"

"Well, good morning, Teresa!"

"Did you hear what I said? That I did it?"

Flo looks out the window. *Did it. Did it.* Then, "Oh!" she says. "You and the cashier and the stars?"

"Yes!"

"Was it fun?"

"Yes!"

"Well, come and have some coffee with me and tell me all about it."

"I have to go to work now, Flo, but I can come and see you at five."

"Just stop by now. One second."

"Okay, but I can't stay."

Flo waits on the front porch for Teresa to pull up outside and then come onto the porch.

"I just wanted to give you something," Flo says.

"What?"

Flo steps forward and hugs Teresa hard.

"Thank you," Teresa says. "For everything."

"You're welcome."

Teresa heads back to her car with what Flo can only call a spring in her step. She looks different. She's acting different. All right, then.

Flo goes back inside to get dressed. Standing out on the porch in her nightie for all the world to see! But she'd been so excited about Teresa she'd plum forgotten she is all but naked.

When she reaches into her dresser drawer for some clean clothes, she finds something she's not thought about for a long time: a newspaper article with a photo of her and Terrence. The page is yellow and delicate to the touch now; she fears unfolding it. But she sits on the side of the bed to read it. After a while, she goes downstairs to enclose the article in plastic wrap.

I want to tell you about the time Terrence won $1,000 from a lottery ticket. These days $1,000 is not such a large sum, but in the 1950s, it sure enough was. When Terrence and I went to collect the money, there were reporters there, and they took pictures. I had known they were going to be there, it was something special to get your picture in the paper then. I put on my best suit and brand-new hose and some high heels, even though I never did like them. I don't know who invented high heels or why, seemed to me like they are never comfortable, and I was always one for dressing comfortable. I wore high heels for Terrence, on account of he liked them. But then, he had to wear ties sometimes and I spect that's worse. At least with high heels you can rest a spell and take the pressure off, but with a tie you must be nigh onto choking all day. But Terrence and I got dressed up and had our picture taken holding the check and then we came home and talked about what we would do with the money. We talked about trips or home decorating or maybe even a new car. And then Terrence said, Flo, I hope you'll be with me on this. I want to give the money to Amos Dooley.

Now, Amos Dooley was a guy worked with Terrence and a sweeter fellow you'd never meet. He was married to a woman named Angela. She and Amos had four kids and don't you know they were the cleanest, best-dressed kids on the block. Angela got all her clothes from the thrift store and from donations from friends and neighbors, we all knew it, didn't anyone look down on her for it. Angela may not have had any money but she sure enough had good taste, and her children looked like they stepped right off the pages of the Sears Roebuck catalogue. And her, too, I saw her once in a tweed straight skirt and a bow tie blouse and she looked almost like a movie star.

So they were nicely dressed and groomed, the whole family, and the house was clean, too, one of those places with the porches swept and the lawn never in need of mowing. But the house was about to fall down, ever in need of repairs, and their car was just a rattletrap that was always breaking down. I knew they had trouble paying their water and electric bills, and sometimes they had the power clean cut off. This was all because Amos had a bad gambling problem. He'd sneak off to the casino, he was in card games all over town, and he bought lottery tickets every week. One time he and Terrence were in a store sold those tickets and Amos bought two and gave one to Terrence. Terrence said he didn't believe in such things and Amos said oh just take a chance, maybe you'll win. He said if he finally won something he would stop gambling, that was a deal he'd made with God.

Terrence didn't think much of that, but he was kind enough not to say anything. Of course by now you've probably guessed what happened. Amos won nothing that day, but Terrence did.

First thing he did was to call Amos and say this money is yours, you bought the ticket, but Amos said no, it's your money, you got it fair and square, I gave you that ticket. He wouldn't take no for an answer. He said tell you what, take me and my family out for a chicken dinner with you and Flo, how about that. Terrence said sure, but it was really bothering him that he won and Amos didn't, and so he asked me about him giving the money to Amos. I have to be honest and say I had a mental image of a pretty new armchair floating right out the window but I said, Yes, go ahead and give it to him. I want you to. We don't need a thing, not really, and they need so much. Terrence said, This is why I married you.

Well, Terrence took Amos out for a drive, saying he wanted to show him a new calf just born over to the Lawson farm that had a perfect star on its forehead, Amos was just a fool for animals. And as they stood at the fence looking at the calf, Terrence gave Amos the money, and he told Amos if he didn't take it, Terrence would be awfully upset. Terrence said, God works in strange ways, right? Well, this is His roundabout way of making sure you honor your promise to Him, because I'm going to keep an eye on you. Terrence said Amos commenced to cry but finally he took the money, and do you know he never did gamble again. So that photo was ever a reminder to me that sometimes when you give away something you get back so much you can hardly contain it. I'm still awfully glad for us giving that money away, Terrence and I, it filled my heart and lifted my soul. And I'll tell you what, this morning I went to the back of my closet where I still have that suit and heels I wore for the photograph and I thought about putting the whole dang outfit on, even rouging my cheeks like I was going all over again to have my picture taken for the paper, Terrence on my arm looking handsome as could be, with his square chin and dimple right smack in the middle. I don't think it's any sin of pride to say we both looked real good on that day. Oh, I hope after I die, I'll be dressed up fine and I'll walk right into Terrence's arms, and I'll bet he'll say, Where have you been? I've been waiting on you, he'll say, and I'll say here I am.

People ask sometimes about what is the measure of a man. I believe I saw Terrence clear on the day I met him, and despite a bad surprise he presented me with and the hard time that followed, I never really deviated from that point of view. No reason to. Read this article which I will put after this page. In it is the measure of Terrence. I feel bad that I have to stick it in a letter, when where it really should go is into a golden vault.

Flo is sitting out on her porch in late morning with her eyes closed, inhaling the scent of the lilacs that grow along the foundation of her house. All her life, whenever she smelled the lilacs of May, she would think, Lilacs are my favorite flower. Then here would come the hussy peonies and she would think *they* were her favorites. Then the bearded irises, with their ruffly purple petals and furry little tongues. ("Hold on," Ruthie had once said, out in Flo's yard and inspecting her stand of irises. "Do these guys drink water like a dog?") Then the deep pink trellis roses came, and then *they* were Flo's favorite. Oh, they were all her favorites, nearly every flower she came across, whether in her yard or a neighbor's.

She hears a footstep and opens her eyes to see Madeline, the mailperson, dropping some things in the tin bucket Flo keeps on the steps to prevent Madeline from having to come all the way up the steps and across the porch. No need for that. Sometimes, on hot days, she leaves a bottle of cold water in the bucket for Madeline; on cold days she might leave an insulated cup of cocoa with many, many marshmallows.

"Good morning, Florence," Madeline says.

"Morning, Madeline. How are you on this beautiful day?"

Madeline raises her chin. "I'll *tell* you how I am. It's good news, how I am!"

"What happened?" Flo asks, and then, "Wait. Do you want a drink of something?"

"No, I've got to make good time today. Because as soon

as my workday is done, I'm being whooshed off to a surprise vacation. It's Bobby's and my thirtieth anniversary, and he's taking me away for two weeks. He said I didn't have to do a thing; he'd even pack my bag for me, to which I of course had to say, 'That's okay, I'll take care of that.' He doesn't need to see my personals."

"Keep the mystery, huh?" Flo says, and Madeline gives Flo a sideways glance and nods.

"But a surprise!" Flo says. "What fun!"

"Well, it's supposed to be a surprise. But Bobby doesn't hear so well, and when he talks on the phone it's like he's using a bullhorn. The other day he told me he was going down to his workbench in the basement to fix something, but I overheard him tell my sister that he and I are going to the Grand Canyon and could she take care of Boodles—he's our cocker spaniel. Oh, I'll act all surprised, I guess I *will* be surprised, really, how can you see a thing like the Grand Canyon right there in front of you and not be all . . . Well, I believe I'll be amazed. *Amazed!* It's something I've always wanted to see, and I'd just about given up ever being able to do it. But I forgot something, which is that as long as you're alive, you should *never* give up on those things you want to do in life. You ever seen the Grand Canyon, Flo?"

"Never have. Only in pictures."

"You ever want to?"

"Oh, sure. But there were things I wanted to do more. I wanted to go to Africa. And also Japan. But I never did." Also Paris, in a way. But also *not* Paris; she had her reasons.

Madeline stands with one hand on her hip, appraising Flo. She's a beautiful woman, dreadlocks down to her butt;

Flo has always admired how she looks. "You still got time for some things," Madeline says. "What about New Orleans? You ever go to New Orleans?"

"Nope," Flo says, and she's starting to feel a little blue. But maybe there are *some* things she's always wanted to do that she still could do.

"Have you ever had a pedicure?" Flo asks Madeline, and Madeline smiles broadly.

"Every other Saturday, ten A.M. Standing appointment. Wouldn't miss it. Once Bobby even got a pedicure with me, but he was sweating bullets the whole time; he couldn't wait to get out of that salon in case someone should walk by and see him in there, a giant man sitting on that pink chair reading *Star* magazine. But men *do* get pedicures now, it's no big thing. And Bobby did admit later that it felt real good, soaking his feet in that little Jacuzzi. Don't you love those little foot Jacuzzis?"

"I've never had a pedicure," Flo says.

"*Never?*"

"Nope. I guess I always thought they were a waste of money. I figured I could surely paint my own toenails."

"Oh, Flo, you should get one. Put it on your bucket list."

"I think I'm too old."

"Ain't no such thing! I seen women using walkers and looking half *dead* come in there, and they look a far sight better going out, too, 'cause their spirits been lifted. One woman I saw last time I went, she was *real* old, and she got glittery gold toes and she was *thrilled* with how it looked; she made Diep take a picture and send it to her grandson. And that woman also had dyed red hair, red like a *crayon*. You ever dye your hair, Flo?"

"Never did. My, I'm beginning to feel boring."

"Well, you could go and get your hair dyed and get a pedicure, *too*."

Flo considers this. "I spect I could."

"What color would you dye your hair?"

"Oh, I don't know. Maybe I'd just get one of those colored streaks, you ever seen those on old ladies, just the one streak?"

"Yes, I have. And I have seen *tattoos* on old ladies, too. One got a full-sleeve parrot!"

"Hmmm," Flo says. "I'll pass on the tattoo."

"I'm sure with you there. You know, in a magazine, I saw a picture of a bride pretty as could be, except her neck and chest were all tattooed! I have to think, what if she comes to regret that? You can't just *erase* tattoos. You have to go in and get tortured all over again to get them off." She looks at her watch. "I'd best get going." She starts down the steps, but turns to say, "Next time I see you, I want to see your polished toes and your dyed hair."

"Uh-huh," Flo says. She wishes she would do that, she does. She rocks back and forth, back and forth, thinking.

Well, hell. Flo gets up and goes inside and calls Lotus Salon, two blocks away. Inside her is a jangly happiness that feels almost like she's nervous. But she's not nervous. Lo and behold there has been a cancellation for 11:00 today, and Flo can get both things done. It just goes to show you. It just goes to show you all kinds of things.

When Flo walks into Lotus, the receptionist, a young Vietnamese woman, looks up. "May I help you?"

Flo says she called earlier, she is the 11:00.

"Oh, yes," the woman says. "I'm Binh. You want a pedicure and hair color?"

Now Flo isn't so sure. But she nods, and Binh says, "Okey-dokey, we'll do the pedicure first. You want to pick out a color?"

"Say what?" Flo cups a hand around one ear.

Binh gestures to a wall of polish. Why, there must be over one hundred to choose from!

Flo goes over to look and finds a lilac color; now, there's an idea. She holds it up and turns around to show Binh. "What do you think?" she asks, and Binh says, "Oh, that's a good one, very popular this time of year."

Flo looks at some of the other colors and sees a bright yellow. Well, isn't *that* cheerful! "What about *this* one?" she asks Binh.

"That's good, too," Binh says.

"Now, Binh. Tell me true. Do you just say they're all good?" Flo asks.

"No. Tangerine Dream, I hate that one. But some people like it so much! I say do what your heart tells you."

Flo gets an idea. "What if I asked you to do one foot lilac and one yellow?"

"I can do that. Also I can alternate toes."

"Alternate toes, you say."

"Yes."

Flo nods. "Let's do that. And what about if we add even *another* color?"

"Whatever you want!" Binh says, and Flo says never mind, just the lilac and the yellow alternating. There will be spring right on her feet. Why, she had no idea this would be so much fun! She starts to walk to the chair where Binh is filling up a tub with water, then pauses.

"You want to add more colors, right?" Binh says, and Flo nods.

"Go for it," Binh says.

Flo chooses three more colors: sky blue, royal purple, and a deep rose pink. There.

She walks over to the chair and Binh helps her up a step so she can sit down in it. It's a big chair! Chairman of the board!

"Okay, we have to take off your shoes and socks," Binh says. She pats her lap and Flo puts her Keds up there and Binh very gently takes off Flo's shoes and socks and then slides her ugly old bumpy feet into the bubbly suds.

"Temperature okay?" Binh asks.

"Oh, yes, very comfortable. I feel like the Queen of Sheba."

"Who is that?" Binh asks.

Flo stares at her. "You know what? I don't really know. I've been saying that all my life and I don't have any idea who the Queen of Sheba was."

The woman in the middle chair in the row reads off her phone: "She was first mentioned in the Hebrew Bible. She gave King Solomon a whole bunch of gifts. Says here a *caravan* of gifts."

"Huh!" Flo says.

"Massage?" Binh asks Flo, holding up a remote control.

Flo doesn't quite know what she means.

"The chair massages you," Binh says.

Flo turns around to look at the back of the chair. "It *does*?"

"If you want."

"Well, how much is it?"

"Oh, nothing! It's free. Some people like it, but some people they don't. Why don't you try?"

So Flo says she'll try it and Binh turns the chair on and Flo says, "Nope, nope, turn it off." When Binh does, Flo says, "That chair would loosen my teeth if I sat there long enough!"

Binh laughs, a soft, bell-like laugh. "We can make it more gentle," she says, and Flo says no, she'll just have her pedicure plain.

"How about a cup of coffee?" Binh says. "Or herbal tea? Or lemon water?"

"For free?" Flo asks, and Binh says yes. *And* she can have a cookie.

"Lord!" Flo says, leaning back in the chair. "Well, then I'll have a coffee and a cookie, too. I'd be a fool not to."

Flo is given her coffee and cookie and the coffee is too strong but the cookie is right good, kind of like a pecan sandy, and she gobbles it up. Binh goes to the reception desk to take a payment and Flo sits still in her chair and looks around at everything: the TV on the wall showing a bunch of overly made-up women who look like they're having a cat-fight, the great number of colorful orchid plants stationed here and there throughout the salon, the rhinestone barrette one of the manicurists is wearing, the woman at the far end of the row of chairs who is engaged in a giggly conversation with the woman painting her toes.

"Magazine?" Binh asks when she returns, and Flo says, "Oh my, no. There is too much to see!"

Binh begins using a pumice stone on Flo's feet and Lord does it tickle! Flo can't keep from laughing out loud. But then comes a gentle foot massage and fragrant lotion and it is just wonderful. Flo closes her eyes and leans back in her chair and she hears Binh talking in Vietnamese to the manicurist next to her. Flo listens for a while, and then she opens her eyes and says, "Say, you're not talking about me, are you?"

"No, no," Binh says. She jabs a thumb toward the woman next to her. "We are talking about her kids."

"Oh," Flo says. "I was afraid you were talking about me."

"No, we're not doing that," Binh says, and picks up one of Flo's feet to gently dry it off.

"How do you say 'feels good' in your language?" Flo asks.

Binh says something and Flo says it back loudly and then all the women in the place have a laugh, including Flo. Well, she only wishes she'd known before how nice this place was.

After Flo's pedicure is done, Binh puts some flip-flops on her and walks her over to the hair-washing station, where a young woman named Debby with a very loud voice washes her hair. Then she is escorted to the chair for hair coloring by Renee.

"What color are we doing today?" Renee asks.

"Well, I don't want to go too radical," Flo says.

"Okay."

"Maybe just a little streak of blue?"

"Sure. Over the temples?"

"Maybe just over one?"

"Of course. Let me show you the shades we have." She brings over a little card with what looks like tassels of hair. Flo points to a turquoise color and Renee says, "Perfect. Now, should we give you a little trim, too?" She runs her fingers through Flo's hair like it *needs* a cut.

"I guess so," Flo says. "Not too much."

"Not too much," Renee says. She takes out her scissors and snip, snip, snip, all of a sudden Flo looks a little better. Then Renee goes to mix the color, and now Flo is excited. She really is. She bets when she goes home she'll go straight to her mirror even though she's already looking into a big, big mirror.

Before she leaves the salon, Flo tips everyone, including the hair washer, who is sitting in back eating her lunch and talking very loudly on the phone. "I KNOW," she's saying. "RIGHT???" When she looks up and sees Flo standing there holding out a ten-dollar bill, she screams. She does, she screams a happy little scream, and Flo thinks, Well that was worth *twenty* dollars!

When Flo pays her bill, Binh says, "You live near?"

"Yes," Flo says. "Two blocks away."

"I'll give you a ride," Binh says. "I have to go to the bank. Come with me to the parking lot, out back."

"Oh, I can walk home," Flo says, and Binh says, "No, I think maybe you should ride with me," and so Flo does.

When she gets home, she realizes she's awfully tired. But she takes the time to look at herself in her bathroom mirror, the nice haircut and the sweet little streak of blue, a little piece of sky, a little piece of heaven right there. She lies down for a nap but first slips off her shoes and socks to look at her wondrous pedicure. There it is. It's hard to see, but it's there. So much of life is like that.

In a little blue cardboard suitcase in the basement, I got something stored that might surprise you. It is the teddy bear I got for Christmas when I was five years old and there he still is. I named him Paddle and I remember I deliberated for a long time about whether I should call him Piddle or Paddle. That seems strange even to me now, but I guess I had my reasons. I took off his blue ribbon and gave him a sheriff's badge I got as a prize in a box of cereal. I've kept him all these years. I guess he looks a sight now but there have been times in my life when I needed him, like when I had a severe flu one year when I was in my sixties, and do you know I really thought I might die. And I told Terrence, too, I said, Terrence I believe I am going to die. I believe I am dying. I was wondering if we should call and get me some extreme unction. And Terrence was sitting on the bed beside me and he said hush now, don't you ever say such a thing, and his eyes got wet. He said you wait right there and he disappeared for a while and when he came back to my bedside he had Paddle. I laughed but I took that old bear and held him smack up against my chest and do you know pretty soon after that I started to feel better.

I used that bear when Terrence died too, and it's a wonder Paddle didn't float away on that occasion when I got him so wet with tears. But he was a comfort always.

I know he'll get tossed, least I sure think so, and if I came upon him unknowing, why I'd toss him too. That bear reminded me about the early days of AIDS when it was still called the Gay Plague, and those young men dying and dying and nobody knowing at that time what to do and Tommy Finton (you remember him, he was your age and a big high school football star) came on home to his parents' house to die and I heard all he wanted was cream of tomato soup and the bear he had when he was a child. Marilee Zimmerman lived next door and she told me she visited him and she said that bear was in the crook of his arm the whole time and it moved her so. I guess that's why I'm telling you about my bear now, you might could give him a fond gaze before he's tossed. I would ask that you leave him in his little suitcase where he has lived all these years, I don't like to think of coffee grounds or the like being dumped on him. You know Terrence once read me out a newspaper article about some gay men who wanted to come home to die and their families didn't want them. I gasped when I heard that, I like to fell out of my chair. That can't be true, I said, and Terrence nodded somber. I looked away from him and stared out across the kitchen and I was so mad that that's all I could do was sit and stare.

Also in the basement, in a Red Owl grocery bag, you'll find the clothes I made for your walking doll. Patti Playpal, I believe she was named, but you called her Vivien Leigh, which I think was because when you asked me who my favorite movie star was I told you Vivien Leigh. You were so tickled to have those clothes for Vivien, nighties where I smocked the bodice, and two pairs of pedal pushers, a black silk evening gown, and a pleated skirt with a black leather belt that Terrence made in his basement workshop. "Is this okay?" he asked when he held it up to show me, and he actually seemed worried like it would be going on a Paris runway. But it was just a perfect little belt with a buckle and little grommets and I liked it so much I wished I could wear it. Anyhow, you just loved everything. I made clothes for that doll until suddenly you were done with her and one day you came over and rang my doorbell and when I answered you handed me a paper bag and said, Here, I'm done with these but my mom said I can't throw them away so I'm giving them back to you.

I confess my feelings were a bit hurt but that's the way things go, everything on Earth is ever changing. I sat on the sofa after you left and I looked at everything I had made and then I put the bag in the basement thinking I'd donate the doll clothes somewhere but I never did. I guess I should have, but it was like I was saving part of you as a little girl.

My friend Claudia Thompson had a big metal trunk that was her husband's from when he was in the Army and it was nigh about stuffed with her children's things and then her grandchildren's—drawings, handprints in clay, Christmas cards with Santa's beard made with cotton balls. She showed me once and I said what are you going to do with all that and she said oh hell, I don't know. I just like to come and sit by it sometimes and rifle through. I think about their little hands, and sometimes I just about come to tears and so then I have to think about how sometimes they were little shits, too.

Say did I ever tell you that one time not long before she died Claudia couldn't get out of her tub and she had to call the fire department—thank God she'd brought her cell phone in with her—and they came and yanked her out. They had to bust open the door and she yelled at them NOW BEFORE YOU COME IN HERE YOU GO AND GET MY ROBE OFF MY

BED AND WHEN YOU COME IN YOU CLOSE YOUR EYES UNTIL YOU CAN THROW IT OVER ME. And they did it. I never did meet a fireman wasn't an awful nice person. They all had a good laugh after Claudia got out safe and sound and she sent them off with some molasses cookies she'd just made.

I wonder why you don't read stories like that in the newspaper rather than the ones make you practically have a heart attack of sorrow.

I got one more thing to tell you about before I'm off to bed even though I'm not much tired. And that is a silver mirror I keep on my dresser. If you turn it over, you'll see there's a little message taped to the top says, *Don't you dare.* That message is one Terrence wrote to me after I'd been doing my usual complaining about getting old and ugly. I can't hardly stand to look at myself in the mirror, I told Terrence one day, and he said don't you talk that way. I spect I kind of frowned and he said don't you know I love how you look now? Ho, I said, that's because when you look at me you remember how I used to look. And he said, To be honest, I suppose there's some of that. But I love how you look because all the years it took you to get those wrinkles you were with me and we were in love and we still are. Well, I said, you sure enough do look at pretty young things, and he said so do you! You look at pretty women more than most men, now why is that? I had to think about that and then I said, I guess I'm just plum mad at them. It felt kind of good to admit it.

"Well, Teresa, I just *loved* meeting your Jim," Flo says. "And you are absolutely right, he is a very nice man. A wonderful man! I know you can see that plainly. And what I can see plainly is that he is in love with you."

"I don't know about *that,*" Teresa says.

"Yes you do."

"I think he was quite taken with *you,* that blue streak in your hair and your *very* cool nails!"

Flo grimaces. "Is it too much?"

"It's wonderful! It's fun!"

Flo crosses her arms and moves the rocker back and forth. The temperature has dropped and she's cold, but she doesn't want to go in yet. "Fetch me that afghan off the sofa inside, would you please, Teresa?"

"Of course."

When Teresa goes into the house, Flo reaches down to her stomach to give it a little rub. Some discomfort there, but not bad. She is too thrilled with what has happened to think about much else.

When Teresa came to see her tonight, she asked Flo if it would be okay if she invited her beau over for just a few minutes, to meet her. Flo just gave her a look, and so Teresa called him to come over.

Jim is a big teddy bear of a man with shaggy gray hair and big blue eyes and the sweetest expression on his face, the kind of man you see on the street and just *know* he's kind. He told Flo about first seeing Teresa, how he just liked her so much right away but felt he had to not give himself away too much, didn't want to scare her. When he said that, he'd taken Teresa's hand and squeezed it, and Flo saw that Teresa squeezed back. New love. People could be 110 years old and it would still be thrilling, both for the couple and for everyone who witnessed their joy. She had a friend who used to say that love was just so that people would procreate, but it's not true. Love is so that people have a *reason*.

Jim stayed for about fifteen minutes, just enough time for Flo to look him over good. And he sure enough passed the test.

When Teresa comes out with the afghan, she arranges it over Flo's lap. "How are you doing, Flo?" she asks.

Flo doesn't answer right away, but then she says, "Last night I was lying right smack in the center of my bed, which I've been doing ever since I had to admit that Terrence wasn't coming back, not even as a ghost, though I had longed for that, if only he could come back and let me hold his ghostly hand and somehow still feel his warmth." She looks over at Teresa and smiles. "We used to hold hands in bed from the beginning of us until his end, and oftentimes I would wake up at some ungodly hour of intense dark and quiet and I would squeeze his hand a little and he would always squeeze back. Always. I don't even know if he was awake when he did that, but he did it and I would fall back asleep, content. In the early days after he died, I swear I used to feel a downward depression on the mattress like he was sitting there to quietly regard me, and it was a comfort. But that stopped after a while and I decided to move to the center of the bed. It is an odd place to sleep if you're used to sleeping on your own side for so long; you feel like you're sneaking into someone's tomato garden. But there I was in the middle of the bed, and I was praying to all the saints in heaven that I would be strong and alone when the time came for me to pass over. I wanted to be *alone*. That's what I prayed for. I thought it would be better that way, no one upset as you left this world behind. Do you think that's strange?"

"No," Teresa says. "I don't think it's strange at all. I'm sure you know stories about some people who seem to wait for the room to be empty before they die."

"Other people, they like to have their family all around them."

"Yes," Teresa says.

"I don't have any family," Flo says. "But even if I did, I just feel I would like to be alone."

Teresa sighs.

"What?" Flo asks.

"I'll miss you. I wish I could ask you to stay longer."

"You can ask me anything."

"*Would* you stay longer? Would you stay as long as you can?"

"I'll see what I can do," Flo says. "In the meantime, can I ask you to do something?"

"Of course."

"You take that love from Jim. Even if it doesn't last. You take it while it's there. It's worth the risk. It's always worth the risk. People don't always believe that. When I was a girl about twelve years old, I had my first boyfriend. He sure was cute. His name was David. Well, we lasted about three weeks, and I nigh about died when he told me he didn't like me anymore. I was crying and crying in my bedroom and my father came in and said, 'What's all this?' I said, 'David doesn't like me anymore, and now I'll *never* find another boyfriend!'

"My father came and sat by me on the bed. I was just snuffling away, my face all swollen up red, me squeezing my big stuffed bear up close and tight, and my father said, 'Yes you will.' I did not believe him. But of course he was right. I suffered a few more heartbreaks, but then I met Terrence."

"And if you hadn't?"

Flo shrugs. "Well, then I wouldn't have. Most likely I would have met someone else. But luckily I did meet Terrence. And now you've met Jim. And I just want you to stick your neck out."

"Looky here," Teresa said, and when Flo turned to her, there was her neck plum stuck out as far as it would go.

I'll sleep tonight, Flo thinks.

In my kitchen cupboard to the right of the sink, in with all the coffee cups, you might notice something. There are two of everything, except for one squat little cup that looks like the bully on the playground—you know, tough because it's short. It's a tan color, similar to ones you've probably seen hundreds of times. But this one meant a lot to Terrence and me, and sometimes we practically fought over who could be the one to have their coffee in there.

We got that cup in 1961 on a fall day with the leaves so gorgeous you couldn't stop looking at them. There was no point in trying to work, was my feeling. And lo and behold Terrence said he felt the same way. So he and I just put on our light jackets and our walking shoes and out we went to take in as much of that beauty as we could hold.

At first, we would say things like Look at that RED! or Oh my goodness doesn't that yellow look just like gold? but finally we stopped talking and we just held hands and walked. We got pooped after a while but we didn't want to go home quite yet so we stopped in the Anytime Diner and got ourselves a meal. It was the kind of restaurant served breakfast anytime, hence the name, and didn't we pile on the pigs in blankets. The coffee there was very good and Terrence said he thought it was in part because of the cups. Do you really think so? I asked and he said why sure, and he drained his cup and then he said he would like to have it, and he made like to stuff it under his jacket. His good sense and his conscience got the better of him and he put the cup back. But he was like a kid looking at the toy he wanted most in the department store window. I told Terrence, Why don't you ask if you can buy a cup and Terrence allowed as how that was a good idea and he asked George the owner could he please buy a cup, he just liked those cups so much and he sure would like to drink coffee from one of them at home. And do you know, George just gave it to him. Go on, take it, he said, I got a lot of them.

Well we walked home and we both of us just kept on looking at that cup like we'd won a trophy. And because there was only one cup, it became even more special.

But here's the thing I really want to say.

I sat for the longest time after we got home, just staring at the cup and thinking two things. One, isn't it amazing what an act of generosity can do to start the wheels turning? And what I did was to make a collection of leaves which I preserved with a glycerin and water bath. I tied a big orange ribbon around it. (And do you know when Terrence came home with that orange ribbon after I sent him to the dime store on an emergency errand because I had a birthday gift wrapped and no ribbon, and then I nearly yelled at him because who would ever use ORANGE ribbon??? It was on sale, he said, and I said well no wonder and he said what and I said nothing.) But that orange ribbon looked as pretty as can be around those leaves and after I had them all arranged I went for a walk with them and I went up to a stranger's house and tied them to the doorknob and then ran away. I felt very excited like a little kid, my heart just a-pumping. And when I got home I had a cup of coffee in George's cup and I thought about how someone would find those leaves and think what the heck?? And they would have a moment of mystery happiness, you know, a surprise where you never find out why and how but you sure enough feel lucky.

The other thing I thought was, it is such a beautiful fall day in 1961 and this day will never be repeated. And it hurt me good but I was also squeezed by happiness. And I rose up from my kitchen chair and I called Terrence to me and I kissed him hard. He flushed, oh can you imagine, but that's the kind of man he was, he flushed and I kissed him again even better and then we repaired upstairs. I hope it doesn't embarrass YOU, me telling you such a thing. But after all we were married. Married down to the pores in our skin, is what I'd say. And I'd also say we knew we were lucky, whatever came our way, we knew it all the time.

Flo is standing at the bedroom window, her mind pleasantly vacant. There is the tree on the boulevard in front of her house, its leaves turning from side to side in the breeze like little boats in rough waters, and that is all. The green, the air, the day.

She looks at the empty street and a memory comes to her from long ago, a time when she knew everyone on the block. Most people were her age—in her forties, then—and in summer kids ran all over the place from morning until the streetlights came on. People seemed much happier then, and more giving. More *willing*. They all watched the same three channels on television, and they all talked about who Jack Paar had had on his show the night before.

One summer Saturday, Flo and Terrence were sitting on the porch getting ready to go grocery shopping—Flo had just finished making out her list—when Terrence up and said something strange. He said, "I'll give you ten dollars if you go out in the middle of the street and bark like a dog."

Flo looked at him, her eyes little slits.

"You know I'm serious," he said.

Flo sighed. He would do things like that sometimes, challenge her to do silly things for a reward of some sort. Recently, when they'd gone to a park for a picnic on top of a gently sloping hill, he'd said, "If you roll down that hill real fast, I'll buy you an ice cream cone." Flo had said, "It would have to be a hot fudge sundae," and he offered his hand to shake on the deal, and so she did roll down the hill real fast and he did buy her a hot fudge sundae. He had wanted to buy himself one, too, but

Flo said no fair, he hadn't done anything to earn it. He said she was right and then looked at her all sad while she was eating so she gave him a good half of hers. He was *fun,* Terrence! But on that day when he told her to bark like a dog, she thought he had gone a bit beyond the pale. She looked out at the street. Ten dollars was not an insignificant amount. She thought of a few things she could buy with it: cold cream, those new nylons that came in an egg—she wanted to try those. She said, "All right, I'll do it. I will. But wait until nighttime so nobody can see me."

"Nope," he said. "It has to be right now."

Flo looked at the street again, blinked a few times, and then rose and walked outside. In the middle of the street, she barked a few times—soft, yippy things—and then she started back for home. One thing she wanted was a new lipstick; she might be able to get two. But from the porch Terrence said, "Nope, it has to be louder so everyone can hear."

Flo stopped walking, her hands on her hips. Then she walked back to the middle of the street and barked loudly: *WOOF! WOOF! WOOF!*

Children in the vicinity stopped playing and came over to stare. And then Edith Peterson came down from her front porch to stand on the curb, and she said, "Whatever are you *do*ing, Flo?"

"Why, I'm standing in the middle of the street and barking like a dog."

"What for?"

"Because Terrence told me if I did it, he'd give me ten dollars. So I'm doing it."

Edith shaded her eyes and looked over at Flo's porch. "If I do it, will he give me ten dollars, too?"

"Only one way to find out," Flo said. She was beginning to have fun. This was much better than grocery shopping.

So Edith came over and stood next to Flo and started barking, and then here came Sally Bensen in her ruffly apron and Ed LaLonde in his battered old slippers and blue cardigan. Next it was Paul and Betty Early, and Paul had actually stopped washing his car to join in and he *never* stopped washing his car once he'd started. But they all just stood there barking and barking and then the little kids joined in, some of them howling like coyotes. And then—Flo could hardly believe it—one of the adults put their arm around another and started a kick line and then they all did that, all except the little kids, who thought it might be more fun just to run around all the adults.

Oh, it was a funny thing. Fun and funny. Someone came out and filmed them with a movie camera; Flo hopes that footage still exists somewhere, all of them so giddy and fully entertained by this impromptu event. Flo doesn't guess that kind of thing would happen now, everyone so busy and locked inside and kind of scared of each other. Why, they would call the police now, if someone stood barking in the middle of the street. People are too serious now, they're all too serious and kind of sad. Well, God bless them. Times are hard now, they are harder than they were before because people are so against each other. Oh, may that come to change. And may it happen soon, before people forget how it *can* be.

She hears the phone ringing and goes down to the kitchen

to answer it. A strange thing happens on her way down the stairs: everything suddenly goes black and white. No color. She blinks a few times—no change. But then the color comes back. Huh, she thinks. I wonder what that was. The body is ever a mystery.

When Flo answers the phone, it is Teresa asking if she can stop by.

"Of course," Flo says. And then, "Do you have a cold?"

"No," Teresa says.

"Well, then . . . are you crying?"

"Not now. I was."

"Why?" Flo squeezes the phone cord. She hopes nothing has gone wrong with Jim.

"I'll come over. I'll tell you then."

Flo heads for the rocker on the front porch, which seems to be her and Teresa's favorite place for talking. Right away, she sees Teresa coming down the sidewalk, her head lowered.

"What happened?" Flo asks as Teresa climbs the steps.

Teresa sits down in the other rocker. "I just . . . I sat this morning with someone whose death was very hard for me."

"Oh, I'm sorry," Flo says.

"You know, I try very hard to keep professional, to not let my personal feelings get in the way of my care. But sometimes I'm more affected than usual by someone's passing, and this was one of those times."

"Who was it?" Flo asks. "If you can tell me."

"A little boy. He was seven. A brain tumor. I sat with him and his parents, and when his breathing changed and his mother knew it would be very soon, she took his face in her hands and she looked into his eyes and smiled at him. She thanked him for being their son and for giving their family so many beautiful things to remember. She said, 'Thank you for being such a special you, we love you always, now and forever.' Then she asked him did he want to go, and he nodded, and she did not cry, she just kept on smiling, and she said, 'Okay, sweetheart, you can go, you go in joy, and we will all be okay. You will live in our hearts forever and we will be with you again.' And then the dad came up and embraced him, and the boy closed his eyes and he was gone. The mother turned to me and she said, 'Did you feel that? This was a holy moment.' I told her, 'Yes, it was.' She said, 'I swear I felt his soul rise. And I knew in that moment he had decided for himself, and in that way he had grown up after all.'"

Flo didn't say anything for a long time, and then she said, "Honestly, Teresa. I don't know how you do what you do."

Teresa nodded. "I know a lot of people feel that way. And it's hard to explain. But the rewards are so great. It *was* a holy moment, Flo.

"I just think . . . there are now and there always were and there always will be such difficult times in life. So difficult. For me, the way to come to terms is not to look away. And if I can help someone, besides . . ." She turns to Flo and her face is earnest.

"Thank you for letting me come over and talk to you. I thought it would help just to be with you, and it did help."

She smiles one of those false bright smiles people do when they're hurting, and then she says she'll be right back.

When she returns, her face is all splotchy. "I'm sorry,"

she says. "I just needed to cry—again. So I went into your powder room and cried a little."

"Well, that's just fine," Flo says. "I think it's a sign of a good friendship if a person feels she can go into your powder room and cry, then come out and *tell* you that. It sets the stage for her knowing that if she should feel teary-eyed again, why, go ahead and bust out crying right in front of your friend. It will only make you closer.

"Why is it, I wonder, that so often it's our weaknesses make us closer? A friend can brag on something good that happened and you can feel happy for them even though you might have to watch yourself for a smidge of jealousy. But when they show a weakness, why there we are right there for them. And that's how I am for you: I'm right here."

"I know you are." Teresa sits back in her chair and takes a good look at Flo. "Are you eating all right?"

"I am."

It's true that she sometimes only has cookies for dinner, but for heaven's sake, what difference does it make now?

Teresa's expression grows serious, almost stern. "And are you thinking positive thoughts?"

"I have always tried to do that."

"What I mean is, are you still thinking specifically that you want to live?"

"Oh, I see," Flo says.

"What?"

"You don't want *me* to die, too. But Teresa, it's different. I'm ninety-two. It's *time* for me to die."

"Not necessarily. People live past a hundred all the time these days."

"I guess some do. But I'm not thinking about whether or not *to* live. I'm thinking about liv*ing*."

Teresa sighs. "I shouldn't be putting any pressure on you to be any way at all. It's just that we've only begun being friends, and I want you to . . ."

Flo lets a few seconds go by and then she puts her hand over Teresa's.

"Why don't we talk about my favorite subject?" she says. "Now. Are you and Jim in love?"

Teresa laughs. "Well, yesterday he asked if I would like to come to his house for dinner. He said he makes darned good chili, did I like chili? I said I did. And so he invited me for tonight and said to wear my best chili clothes. But I don't know, Flo . . ."

Flo says, "*What* don't you know?" And she is a little cranky because one thing gets her going is when people turn away the possibility of love, especially when they're lonely, and Teresa *is* lonely, you can see it plain as day. It's just so odd how sometimes the loneliest people are the ones most scared of fixing that loneliness. But then Teresa asks in a tiny voice, "What are chili clothes?"

"*That's* what you're worried about? Mercy, just wear your dungarees and wrap a kerchief cowgirl-style around your neck. Maybe some red lipstick and blue eyeshadow. And if you like the chili, say, 'Why, this is slap your pappy chili!'"

"That might be fun," Teresa says, and Flo can see her eyes commence to twinkle. But then she says, "He is starting to go bald quite a bit in the back."

"Have a good *time* with him!" Flo says. "And tell me everything that happens, unless it's too personal. Although if it *is* personal, I might pay attention better. I like hearing details so personal they make you stop chewing."

Teresa looks at her watch and says she'd best be going, she has to visit some more clients.

"Hold on," Flo says, and she gets up and goes into her bathroom for her rosewater bathing solution. When she returns to the porch, a little out of breath, she hands the bottle to Teresa. "Here," she says, "you take a bath in this before you put on your chili clothes." She plops back down in her chair.

"This is brand new!" Teresa says, and Flo says, "I have more. Now, listen to me: if you take a bath in this he will be crazed by desire."

"Ha ha," Teresa says, but she is all serious.

"Ha ha," Flo says back, just as serious.

Teresa starts down the steps, but then she turns around. "Can I come and see you tomorrow?"

"I'll be here," Flo says, and hopes it's true.

She stares out at the street, but she doesn't see it. She sees instead the bluebonnets she grew up with in Texas, the piercing beauty of them. She sees the breeze moving through willow trees like it's combing the trees' hair. She hears her mother calling her home; her mother used to stand out on the back stoop and bang her wooden spoon against a saucepan, and didn't Flo come a-running like there'd be something new when she got there. There was never anything new. Only a bath with the floating Ivory and then clean pajamas, same as always. Still, the call to home. The turning back of bedclothes to receive a tired body, that last letting go before sleep. She wonders if there's anyone else who feels a communion of spirit as they are drifting off, if anyone else feels what you might call a *presence* helping to persuade you into rest. Not that Flo ever needed much persuasion. She has always gone gladly into sleep, for the promise of the new day.

It's funny, Flo thinks. All of us waking up every morning ignorant of all that may befall us. Befall or enrich or enlighten or who knows what. It's no surprise to her that especially as she got older she began to feel more acutely the need to be careful. As if you could control anything. Life was a bucking bronco. If you got on to ride, you took your chances.

She thinks about Teresa getting ready to go to Jim's house for dinner, and she hopes with all her heart that it goes well. She wants so much for Teresa to understand that the love in the world is for *her,* too. She wishes she could give her a kind of confidence she doesn't think Teresa has ever had; she wishes she could *give* her that, same as handing over a plate full of food: *Here. Take it.*

So much of a person's life can be bound up with trying to get things, when it turns out that the best thing is *giving,* and Flo doesn't think she did enough of that in her life. Sometimes it was just pure laziness, sometimes ignorance, but mostly, she realizes now, it was a kind of doubt that she *should* give something: a gift, kind words, an offer to help. What if that help wasn't wanted? What if she was seen as interfering? What a foolish fear! She wishes more than anything else that in these last days she can give something. You got to give. It's like miniature stars thrown over your shoulder: little pieces of light that can land and change the atmosphere, even if you don't see it happen. You got to try. She wishes she had been bolder in this life. Maybe she should have on her tombstone: *Here lies a shy woman ever in love with the world. She should have shown it more.*

On my closet shelf, on the right-hand side, is a green canvas gift box of three small albums labeled Dreams, Journeys, and Travel that I never did put any pictures or anything else in. It's just all tied up and waiting like the day I got it at some thrift store, and do you know the person who had it before me left it empty, too. When I bought it I thought, I'm going to fill those albums up, but then it seemed like I wanted to imagine things that might be put in there more than doing them. It's like when you have a dream and it's like a sparkly floating evening gown but then you write it down and it becomes a faded housedress on a wire hanger. So I would look at the album labeled Dreams and I'd sure enough feel dreamy unto magical. I would look at Journeys and think about how a person gets from here to there, like a friend of mine who was scared of even going to the Piggly Wiggly and then she up and moved to Positano, Italy. She used to talk about Positano, Italy, she used to say that if she could ever work up the courage to travel she would go there. She had pictures of it that she looked at over and over. It looked like a place you'd make up but it was sure enough real. But she moved there! By herself! She sent me a postcard saying I DID IT and that was the last I heard from her. Whenever I thought of her, I was filled with wonder and a fair amount of envy. Fact, one time Terrence came out and I was sitting on the back porch with my apron on, my hands folded in my lap. He asked what I was doing and I said, "Nothing, but

I was wondering what makes for the way your life goes." It was too big a question to ask Terrence, we were fixing to eat dinner in a few minutes, I remember I had made chicken-fried steak and mashed potatoes and green beans right out of the garden. And I thought maybe I'd talk to Terrence later about my big question but it faded away. We both liked chicken-fried steak so much we were content to eat it in silence and then watch Ed Sullivan. My question didn't matter anymore, it slipped right through the colander.

Now, in my bottom dresser drawer, next to your letters all bundled up, you will find something embarrassing. It is an empty Mrs. Butterworth and an empty honey container in the shape of a bear. Terrence and I were having breakfast one day and the honey and the syrup were on the table, and I started talking like I was Mrs. Butterworth and Terrence started talking like he was Mr. Bear. And do you know we said things that we never would have said otherwise, fanciful things, funny things, things I'd just flat out call dear. And seemed like we needed those props to say those things, so I washed out the containers and whenever I needed a special talk with Terrence, why, I'd haul them out. I'd put on my Mrs. Butterworth voice and say, "Dear?" And here would come his gruff bear voice saying, "What is it, my little plumpling?" It was just silly stuff, Ruthie, the kind of thing that we'd never want to admit we did, but we relished our play time, seems like people might never outgrow that need for play to lift them up and away for a bit. After Terrence died, I came home to an empty house that was changed forevermore, the air so heavy around me it was like a coat. And I took off my black hat and my black shoes and I started to take off my black dress but then I kept it on. I went to the dresser drawer and knelt before it, and I pulled out Mrs. Butterworth and Mr. Bear. And then I asked Mr. Bear where he was and there was a long silence, of course. But just when I was going to put the things away, there came a touch to my cheek, I believe it was real, Ruthie, a touch to my cheek, and I felt the promise in it that I would be with him again. And when I took off my black dress and put it on the hanger, it slid off and onto the floor. Terrence never did like me in black.

Oh, here's something that might surprise you, Ruthie. I got brass knuckles in my nightstand. I got them after I started living alone. I figured the bad man would break in and I would hold them up and say, Don't make me use these. And he would bust out laughing so hard he would lose his menace and maybe I'd fix him some coffee and tell him to mend his ways. And maybe he would.

There's a footprint in concrete round back by the cellar door that I want to call your attention to. Terrence stepped in wet concrete by mistake and didn't he have a fit, seeing as how he messed up the job someone had just finished. Finished and warned us not to step in. But here came Terrence out to inspect the man's work right after he left. A man may not know a single thing about how to do something, but when a skilled workman does it for him, why, here he will come to inspect it afterward. Well, Terrence was bending over to have a good look and he slipped on wet grass and there was his footprint smack dab in the slab. We thought about calling the man back to fix it, but it would have cost too much so I said let's just call it a happy accident, there you will be long after you're gone. Those were the days neither of us believed we would ever be gone, not really. But there's that Terrence footprint. After he died, I would sometimes lay flowers in it. And I would see him all over again with his foot slid in the concrete, flustered and angry but laughing, too. His hands on his hips, staring over at me in his "Dang it!" way.

Let's see what else. On a table in my living room is a pretty blue bowl and in it are little rocks that you presented me with one day saying they were magic beans. Go ahead and wish on them, you said, and I did. Not only then, but most every day, it made me feel good. On the same table, there's a note in a frame where the print has faded so you can hardly read it but it says, "Roses are red, violets aren't green, being with you is like living a dream." That was from Terrence on our first Valentine's Day together as a married couple and I just felt like it ought to be framed.

Flo is doing a slow walk around her house to see if there is anything else she should tell Ruthie about. It's raining, the kind of heavy, messy rain that coats the windows with sheets of water and turns the view outside into an indistinct watercolor. She hopes it quits soon; she has arranged for Mildred and Teresa to meet at Mildred's house. It's not far, of course, but Flo has never been one of those love-to-walk-in-the-rain types. No. It's a big fat nuisance to walk in the rain.

She stands before the living room bookcase and bends down to scan the titles. Well, for heaven's sake, there is *Mrs. Mike.* She remembers now she read it just before she and Terrence were married. Flo was in such a romantic state in those days, and this book just added to it. It is about a sixteen-year-old girl from Boston who marries a handsome Canadian Mountie and it nigh onto made Flo swoon. She still remembers lying in bed waiting for Terrence on their wedding night, thinking that both the girl in the book and she had had a lucky break, finding the men they did.

She pulls the book off the shelf and sees a little paper bag hidden behind it. She opens it to find three twenty-dollar bills and a photograph of a particular locket Flo had seen in the paper years ago and had cut out just to look at. It was so pretty, fourteen-karat gold filigree and a few little diamonds here and there. She stuck it in the napkin holder to keep for a while, but it disappeared after a few days. She figured Terrence had tossed it and that was okay with Flo, she was done drooling over it. But now she realizes Terrence had been saving to buy it for her, and he'd kept that picture so that he'd get the right thing.

What to do with this? She doesn't want to use the money to buy anything because it seems that would somehow be wrong. It would dishonor Terrence's intentions. He wanted it to be a lovely surprise.

She goes to the kitchen and writes a note: *To whoever finds this: Use this money to buy something nice for someone who is not suspecting it.* Then she puts the little sack back and pulls the book out just slightly from where it had been. A clue. Isn't it fun to think about who might find it, and what they might buy?

It's time to go to Mildred's, and luckily the rain has stopped. Flo makes her way carefully down the steps and avoids the puddles to get to Mildred's house. While she doesn't like walking *in* the rain, she sure does like the smell *after* a rain, and the way the birds come back out and fluff up their feathers like they're miffed.

When Flo arrives at Mildred's house, Teresa is already there, sitting in the living room, where Mildred has set out a silver tea service. And someone else is there, too: Mimi the librarian. All of the women are a little dressed up. Mildred is wearing a white blouse and a long flowered skirt. Mimi has on a red dress with white polka dots, and she has a red scarf tied artfully around her neck. Flo has never seen Teresa in a dress, but she's wearing a navy blue one today, and she's wearing a yellow scarf tied the same way; Flo thinks Mimi might have taught her how to do it.

"Well, isn't *this* nice?" Flo says, sitting down in one of the comfortable armchairs.

"Have a cookie," Mildred says. "I didn't make them, so they're good."

"I will," Flo says, and she hopes Mildred won't notice if she doesn't eat.

"We're talking about whether love at first sight is real," Mimi says. "So far, it's a divided opinion. Guess who doesn't believe in it and who does?"

"Teresa doesn't," Flo says.

"Neither does Mimi," says Mildred. "But I do. How about you, Flo?"

"Course I believe in it. I experienced it."

"Me, too," says Mildred. Then, laughing, "*Lots* of times."

"How are things going with Jim?" Flo asks Teresa, and then covers her mouth.

"It's fine," Teresa says. "I told them all about him. They've been giving me some good advice."

"Oh, they have, have they?" Flo asks, a mite jealous.

"Sure," Mildred says. "I was telling Miss Cynic here that there *are* ways to keep love alive."

"I've read that you should introduce yourself to each other every day," Mimi says. "Meaning don't assume that a man who has come to know you keeps *on* knowing you. Or you him. Because you both change, over time. You need to keep on checking in with each other."

This reminds Flo that she must write to Ruthie about that one last thing. She'll excuse herself soon to go home and tend to that.

In the meantime, look how animated and comfortable Teresa is with Mildred and Mimi. When Flo is gone, all of them will each have a lovely new friend. Flo feels a kind of soft landing inside, a kind of laying down of satisfaction mixed with just a little sorrow.

I'm up from a long nap and out on the porch and it's evening time, the light not quite drained from the sky. Dusk, I guess it's called, but I always did prefer evening time. Dusk is too short and choppy a word for such a languid time of day. It's a Northern word when you need a Southern one. But whenever this time of day comes, I turn on my porch light. It's not for safety, whoever did believe some puny porch light would scare off anything? No, I turn it on to offer a beacon against the darkness. And I guess I turn it on for Terrence, same as I used to when he was alive and out working, and long about this time I would miss him so, and I would turn on the light to welcome him back to me. Still do miss him, as I must have made clear. Still do. I turn on the porch light most nights and it gives me a bit of hope, unreasonable though it may be. And whenever I flick the switch, I always think of the lyrics in that beautiful song, "Jesse": ***And I'm leaving the light on the stairs, No I'm not scared, I wait for you.***

I believe I have to stop telling you about this and that, and that and this. I'll end up turning 105 and still be writing this letter. Maybe that's why I am writing this letter! Here's my guardian angel tapping her watch, her feathers likely to plum dry out and I'm saying hold on, one more thing. But you know I don't think she'd be angry, I think she'd understand, maybe because she too was reluctant to let go until she finally came to that moment of readiness. I spect I might be ready but for this stubborn holding on to so many things, light moving up my kitchen wall like my own personal sundial, and words in the newspaper that I can't hardly read anymore but there they are dutifully reporting. And I love receiving my new friend Teresa and watching my old friend Champ lumber over for his visit. Oh, Ruthie, it's true that at the end everything becomes precious. Thus I tell you stories about certain things in my house, how you should at least have a meet and greet before tossing. I'm sure you've had enough and I understand.

But if you will permit one last thing.

I was raised Catholic, and I had to go to confession every Saturday. It used to nearly wear me out trying to remember my sins, so when I was about nine years old, I came up with a list of initials to help me remember my sins: PGFJC. Forgot my morning or evening prayers, gossiped about people, fought with my best friend, got jealous of others, didn't always pay attention in church. Those were my sins, I still remember. It seemed bad enough to me, but when I think about what people might confess these days! Some of those people, if they told their sins, the priest might fall right out of the booth. There's so much violence and hatred in the world and if I didn't have the inconvenience of dying coming up, I might just try to do something about it. On a grassroots level. Why, I'd put a kindness booth on the sidewalk in front of my house if I thought I could get away with it. A kindness stopping off point, you come down the street and stop in front of my booth and I tell you something to make you feel good. Or give you a donut or a flower, your choice. I wish I could do that, Ruthie, just thinking about it makes me feel better. I never saw an angry person didn't respond at least a little to kindness. It reminds me of this one dog I used to pass on my walks, every time I went by he'd yank at his big old metal chain and bark and bark and snarl nasty. I used to hustle up to get by him but then one day I stopped and stood before him and I said real soft, Are you a good boy? He stopped barking and just looked at me. Are you? I said. I'll bet you're a good boy on the inside. He cocked his head like dogs do. You can't hardly not like a dog when they do that. So I ventured a step closer, and he watched me with danger and fear in his eyes, and the fear is what surprised me. You're a good boy, I told him, and every day from now on I'm going to stop and talk to you and maybe you'll let me pet you someday. I tried taking one more step closer but he commenced his usual barking and growling and pulling hard on his chain so I walked away. But when I was some distance down the sidewalk, I chanced to look back at him, and he was looking after me and I figured he was thinking, We'll see, old lady. We'll see. And I figured he might lie on the rug in his living room when he went in, and put his chin on his paws and just think things over.

Well, once again I have gone on and on about something that is not the thing I want to talk about. I want to end this letter (FINALLY, I'll bet you're saying!) by telling you a very important thing I've kept from you. And that is what I was burying in the backyard all those years ago.

Let me see how best to proceed. From the beginning, I guess. And the beginning is that I once came upon Terrence's open jewelry box. I was surprised to see it open. He was careful about always keeping it locked to guard against theft. I once teased him about that, saying that all the thief would have to do is lift up the jewelry box and stick it in his gunny sack.

Terrence said, Well at least he'd have a hard time getting it open after he got it home. We'd been out to a kind of fancy party the night before, and Terrence had been digging in his jewelry box, trying out cufflinks. He was not a vain man, but he did like a nice set of cufflinks and whenever he wore them, they would have to be the right ones. So I was standing in the bedroom with my coat on telling Terrence to hurry up, we going to be really late, and he kept coming out with this pair of cufflinks or that to ask me about and finally I grabbed him by the arm and said, Let's GO, the ones you have on are FINE.

We got home very late and Terrence got up early in the dark and went to work. Later, when I went into the closet to hang up the shirts I'd ironed, I saw the open jewelry box. I was scared at first, thinking, Oh Lord, a thief came when we were sleeping. But all the cufflinks were there, there didn't seem to be anything missing. Then I saw something sticking out from between the liner and the side of the box. I thought, What is this, a note? It wasn't a note. It was half a dollar bill. And you know, I got a prickle run up my spine and I knew this thing had some import. That night at dinner, I showed it to him. I said, What's this? He hesitated just for a second and then he said where did you find that? In your jewelry box, I said. You forgot to lock it last night. He reached for it and I held it back. There was a deadly silence and then he said, That is from a long time ago. It is something a friend of mine gave me. And I still want to keep it, so give it back. I gave it back but Why? I asked. Why do you want to keep it?

Don't you have some old things you kept that are not my business? Terrence said. I did have some old love letters but they were no secret. He knew I kept them tied up in a blue ribbon in a cigar box that I kept on the closet shelf. He could have read them, but he didn't, and I guess I was glad. But this secret that he had kept from me made me uncomfortable. I felt like a cold wind was blowing through me. Still, I decided to forget about it.

And I did, until one day years later when a letter came to the house addressed to Terrence from Paris, France. It wasn't securely sealed and that was too much temptation for me and I opened it. Inside was half of a dollar bill. The other half. And there was a note that said, "For so many years I have waited for nothing. Au revoir."

Well, I made an apple pie for dinner and after we'd eaten it for dessert, I told Terrence, Let's go in the living room. Not the porch? he said. We were in the habit of sitting on the porch after dinner which you well know because you used to join us sometimes to show us your drawings or a new toy you'd gotten or your scabs. I never did see a child so interested in showing off scabs.

Anyway, me and Terrence in the living room. I straightened my housedress beneath me. I cleared my throat. Uh-oh, Terrence said. And I said Yes, uh-oh, and my heart was torn between love and rage. I held up the half of a dollar bill that had been in the letter. He sighed and said, This is about that half of a dollar bill again? I nodded and then I held up the envelope and said, But it's about this half of the dollar bill, and I handed him the envelope. He looked at it and read the note inside and got quiet and clasped his hands and hung them between his knees. His head was lowered and his shoulders sunk down. Then he looked up and he said, I'm going to tell you everything. I don't really believe that you need to or should share every cotton-picking thing in a marriage but I have shared every cotton-picking thing with you but this. And maybe it's time, it's been over thirty years.

He sat back in his chair and breathed and breathed. And then he asked me, Could we go out on the porch to talk? He wanted to change the channel to be more normal. I said I thought that what we were about to talk about was too private for that. I'll talk low, he said, and I said well I might not. He looked over at me and smiled but it was such a weary smile, so careful and sad, and never mind that I was so mad at him, it made me feel sorry for him. We can go out on the porch after, I said. Just tell me. And tell it all.

Well, he did tell me all. He started at the very beginning, how she had rushed out of a crowd of French people welcoming the Americans into Paris and kissed him. Lots of women were doing that, rushing up to soldiers and kissing kissing kissing them, they were so joyful, so teary relieved, so grateful that Paris had been liberated and that the War in Europe was over. He said he didn't want to think much of her kiss, he and I so newly married and him so deep in love with me. He said she didn't want to think much of it, either. But something happened for both of them, when they shared that kiss. It hurt me bad, Ruthie, to hear him say "both of us" referring to him and another woman. There I was waiting at home for him, minding my p's and q's, just dying for him to come back. But he and Simone had that kiss and then he said they just stood there looking at each other and then she took his hand and led him away from the crowd. He said he was sorry to tell me but in that moment after the kiss he felt alive after he had been feeling dead inside for so long. What we had been through, Flo, he said, that awful war, what we had been through and—

I interrupted him then, I said I get the point, go on. He told me out all the rest in a rush. How they went to her apartment where she said she had never felt something like this, what she had felt instantly for him, and she didn't care that he was married. He said he had wanted to say that he cared, but then one thing led to the other . . .

Tell me, I said, cold. Tell me what led to what. Tell me in detail.

Oh, Lord, the look he gave me, Ruthie. But he did tell me. They went out onto her balcony with glasses of champagne. They toasted. Then they came in and commenced kissing, she started it but he went along, he went right along. They went to bed, it was late afternoon, and they didn't get out of that bed until the next morning and then that night they were back in it. This went on for three days and then Terrence was scheduled to come home. He said he had very deep conversations with her and I guess he heard the silent question in my head which was what about our conversations and he said their conversations came from what they'd been through in the war and it was hard to explain. But Simone said that they were soulmates. She said that her name meant heard by God, and she truly believed that God had at last heard her entreaties for a love higher than any she had known or expected to know, and Terrence the American had been sent to her. There he was. But he was married. And he was leaving. On the day Terrence left, he took a dollar bill out of his wallet and he tore it in half and told her, Here, you keep this half and I'll keep the other, it's light, we can always carry it. She said, This is the end, then, and Terrence said no he needed time, but he told her take this torn bill as a symbol of their togetherness.

By now my heart felt squeezed to death, but I had demanded the truth. I asked Terrence, Did you think about divorcing me and marrying her instead? He waited a while to answer and then he said, At first, I did. But on the plane ride home I came back to you, Flo, to you and me together. I vowed to forget about her. But the truth is I never did. And once or twice a year I would call her. And . . .

Then came a silence so deep and I knew. I said, You have a child with her. He said, I do. A son.

I lost all my air inside. I couldn't hardly move. I believe both of us were hurting real bad at that moment. But then I said, Let us go out on the porch and not talk any more just now. I believe I need the open sky to hold all I'm feeling. Terrence said, I'll stop all communication with her, and I said all right but didn't her sending you the half dollar mean she was stopping with you? He said he supposed that was right. I asked did she marry someone else and he said yes. So at least I had that.

We went out on the porch and I near about rocked a hole in the floor. But I had made that vow that if Terrence came back home to me after the war, nothing would ever make us part. Nothing. So what I decided under the evening sky that turned velvet black with only the light of the stars coming out is that I would forgive him. I knew it would take time, but I would forgive him. And I'm so glad I did. He offered to throw that dollar bill away and I said no, I said it represented an important part of his life and he should not deny it. Keep it, I said, only don't put it somewhere where I might find it again.

He reached for my hand then, Ruthie, and I took it and it was warm and solid and it was Terrence's hand, and he was there with me.

Now. I spect you think you know what I'm going to say here. Stand by your man, and that awful thing in the movie *Carousel* where Julie Jordan tells her daughter that when her husband hit her, it didn't hurt at all. I bout threw my popcorn at the screen when I heard that. No, if a man hits you, you got to go. But that's not what your man did, Ruthie, I'm sure of it. And all your complaints about your Jonathan that day we took a walk together? I'm sorry, but they don't add up to much. They are things you can fix, seems like small things can assume such a great size in a marriage, it's ridiculous. Why, one time I got so mad about Terrence's being late for dinner two nights in a row (he didn't appreciate all I did for him, he thought I was his maid), anyway I got so mad I thought that's it, I'm getting a divorce, and then I imagined being in front of the judge and saying well he was late for dinner two nights in a row and the judge smacking his forehead and saying go home, you two, get out of my courtroom.

Oh I am tired now, Ruthie, but I'm going to finish. This is what I'm telling you. The things you get mad at about your husband, sometimes it's not him you're mad at, sometimes it's you. Sometimes you're just about boiling over with a frustration you can't quite put your finger on and there is your husband nearby and why not put it all on him. But what you need to do is talk to him. Let him in. And come to forgiveness of him and you.

I believe that forgiveness is our holiest sacrament. You know my friend Teresa told me the three most common things that people say to others on their deathbed. They are I forgive you, I hope you forgive me, and I love you. In the grandest scheme of things, what else matters more? We need not to sanction bad behavior. Just forgive it. And admit that Lord, we are all messes sometimes. Let us strive for better. Let us strive for good.

I got more to say but I am going to have to lie down. Here is my prayer, to wake up one more time so that I can tell you out the rest. What I did besides forgive. What is buried by the roses.

Flo walks slowly over to open the shade to look out at the street and her heart is heavy with love for all that is out there, but it is hard to see, mostly what she sees is light.

She goes down the hall and into the bathroom to wash up and to get ready. Hard to see! She feels for her little pot of rouge in the drawer and rubs some on her cheeks. Too much? She looks in the mirror. Can't tell. She feels for her lipstick and puts some on.

Back to her room and she finds what she wants in the closet. And then she slowly dresses and makes her way downstairs. It's hard to make it down the stairs. But she wants to finish. She remembers a blind man she met named James Monroe, who told her he could still write letters because he put a ruler on the page and wrote the best he could above it. And it was good enough. People could read it. Flo goes to the silverware drawer and feels for a knife to act as a ruler. Then she stations herself at the kitchen table and all the heaviness she has been feeling begins to lift.

I was telling you about Terrence and Simone. After Terrence and I came back into the house that night, he threw the letter and the envelope away. We went to bed and lay in each others' arms, sorry and grateful and sore and tender all mixed up together. In the morning, after Terrence went to work, I fished that letter out of the garbage and I wrote to Simone. It was a short note saying I'd heard about her and I knew she'd had a baby by Terrence and although it may sound funny could I ask for a picture of him. I told her I had not been able to have children and I would like to know what Terrence's son looked like. I wouldn't say it was a nice letter, but it wasn't mean, either. I left it unsealed and I went to the post office and got a box and the little key and I added the return address to my letter and mailed it and then I waited. I told myself that I would wait three months and if I didn't get an answer I would turn in the key to the post office box and that would be the end of that. But I had to try because I knew otherwise I would wonder all my life about that child.

As it happened, I only had to wait two weeks. On the day I got a return letter, I had gone to the post office for stamps and then stopped as usual to look in the box. There it was, a little square envelope, and I opened it right then and there and it was a card with birds and flowers on it, a right pretty card. And there was a picture of a young man in there, and he was handsome as all get out and he had Terrence's eyes and dimples exact. I stared at that photo and then I read the note that came with it, which I have memorized from reading it so many times. It said, Here is the photograph you requested. I am sorry for your pain but I am not sorry for Jean-Claude. I hope you are not angry at Terrence after all these years for what happened between him and me. He is a man who is part angel, I saw that right away. It was the end of the War, we were swept up in it. But I am sorry for your pain and mine. I love my husband, but I will never forget Terrence. Such things happen. I wish you well.

I brought her letter home and hid it in an old Kotex box and I looked at the picture of Jean-Claude many times. And after a few days I wrote Simone back, thanking her for honoring my request. And then she wrote back to me, and I to her. I did not tell Terrence about our correspondence; I did not want him to think about Simone anymore. I thought for the sake of us I would keep this between me and Simone. And it's funny, she and I seemed to need to talk in this way. Maybe it was a kind of exorcism. She told me a lot about Jean-Claude, how he was a doctor and a father himself now. She told about life in France and I told about life in America; she had never come to visit the country. Oh, we shared quite a few letters, there was a flurry of mail, and then after a while, it stopped. We said our own au revoirs. And I took her letters and the photo she'd sent of Jean-Claude and I buried them. I didn't want them in my house anymore but I didn't want to throw them away. I thought about showing the picture to Terrence, but I didn't want us to go through all of that again. So I buried them in a pretty rosewood music box I found at a thrift store, and you can dig them up and read them if you want and see how sometimes something that seems unforgivable isn't. I don't think it's too strong to say that Simone and I became friends, in a way.

Now I want to say something else.

You were ever a hot-headed person, Ruthie, I think you'll admit to that. Your poor high school boyfriends, you put them through the mill. Now you know I love you but you are a hot-headed person. And I'm going to tell you to think, Ruthie. To think hard before you bust up what is probably a good marriage. I don't know why marriage doesn't come with a warning sign, because it is hard. But if you can overcome something together, you will be stronger. Take your own man on your own front porch. Ask him to open his creaky heart, and you open yours, Ruthie, without vengeance. See what happens.

Oh, Ruthie. In some ways the world is so vast and unknowable, all the things in the water and in the sky and all the things walking along the crust, mostly not minding their own business—man or beast, seems like we seek to interact one way or another. In other ways, though, the world seems very small, very small and dear, like something you could put in your pocket.

I am sorry to leave with summer coming, all the little kids running breakneck up and down the block, the little girls with their tops off just like the boys. I remember when you were about eight years old and your parents told you that you would have to start wearing a top, you were too old now not to. I heard you yell GOD A'MIGHTY, WHY?? and you got a spanking for your language. Afterward, you came stomping over to my house and sat on the front porch step and said I do NOT want to go along with THAT one, it is stupid and when they aren't looking I'm taking my top right back off. I don't even have any titties. Then you asked would I like a mudpie you'd made earlier that morning. Of course, I said, and you brought over a mudpie decorated with a dead moth which you said was pretty and there was no need for it to go to waste. But don't eat this, you said and I said I would not. It's just for lookin', you said and then you sighed in that forlorn way you sometimes had. I said I had butter brickle ice cream and we could eat that and you said yes ma'am and asked if you could have a cone, too. We ate our cones and ice cream and you were near the bottom of your cone when you said, Well, I can't eat another bite!!! but then you finished it. I believe you had just wanted to say that, maybe you heard someone else say it and it sounded fine to you. You did that sometimes, just quoted something you'd heard. Cash on the dollar, you once said, and I said what does that mean and you said heck if I know and skipped off.

Flo rubs her hands, her eyes. Then she continues.

I would say you needed me, Ruthie, and I needed you too. It's gone on a long time, our needing each other in one way or another, even now. I guess especially now.

I wish you would right about now show up and knock at my door and I would shuffle on over and let you in. I would put this stack of papers in your hands and I would kiss your cheek just like I always do when I first see you again. Kiss your cheek and hold your face between my hands to take a good look at how you have changed and how you have not. I don't guess I'd have to say a word. Course I know that's not going to happen so I'll just leave this letter (I wonder would it get in the Guinness Book for the longest letter) setting here on the kitchen table and hope it gets to you. I have made arrangements for my new friend Teresa to mail it and I believe I can trust her.

A breath. Two.

And now I guess I will say goodbye, Ruthie. I'll miss you. Well, probably not because I'll be in a different zone but you know how it is, people all the time saying what they'll miss when they die. That Norah Ephron said she'd miss a certain kind of bath salts. And pie. I'll miss hot cross buns every Easter and the flowers bowing in their gardens in the late afternoon and snow that looks just like falling lace. I'll miss the pretty piano music comes on the radio for free. I'll miss the rumble of thunder and rain-mottled sidewalks and the tall green trees. I'll miss the surprise of what each day might bring which we so often forget about, those surprises that can delight us. I once saw an ant walking down the street and his shadow was beside him and it made my heart expand like an accordion and to this day I still can't really say why. And there are surprises that come unexpectedly that can save our lives, too, there are! An idea you'd never thought of before that pulls you out of the drowning pond.

Well, I wish everyone well, everyone I know and everyone I don't know. And I wish everyone peace, a quietness of spirit that we don't seem to have enough of, but maybe if we all hope for it, lo and behold it will come to pass. Wouldn't that be something. Like a strange and brilliant light in the sky that zings the place that needs zinging.

Oh, I just remembered one last thing! There is a big box in

Dear Teresa McNair,

Thank you so much for sending me Flo's letter. I was so very sorry to hear that she had died, even though she had prepared me for it when we last spoke a few months ago. At that time, she had not yet been diagnosed, but she had not been feeling well. She lived a good long life, and I suppose that's some compensation for those of us who loved her.

I am deeply appreciative of Flo leaving her house and its contents to me. It came as a complete surprise, though I know Flo and Terrence had no relatives or children, and that in some respects Flo thought of me as her daughter.

Flo's house is very important to me, but I cannot manage things in person—my husband and I are in the process of buying a new house here in California. There is a realtor there named Sandy Bellman (she owns the self-named agency) whom I have contacted, however, and she assures me that all the necessary paperwork for selling Flo's house can be done electronically. Sandy will also manage an estate sale.

In her letter, Flo told me about the significance of some things that are in her house. It was beautiful to read, and I am returning the letter to you so that you can read it, too. There are a few things I will ask Sandy to send me: Flo's silver spoons, her Mrs. Hen mug, her old teddy bear, her pearls, her embroidered dishtowels, and the little white box wrapped in red ribbon that has an elastic band inside—she kept it in her kitchen drawer. If you think there is something you (or anyone you know Flo liked) might want, please contact Sandy and ask her to let you into the house before the estate sale—I believe you must have been a good friend, and that Flo would want you to have anything you like. There is a good woolen blanket that she mentions. I wonder if a shelter could use it?

I wish I'd have been able to offer a final thanks to Flo for what she gave to me as a child growing up next door to her, and as a friend to me for all my life. She was ever a kind and generous person—and a very wise one. I wish she could know how much she helped me by writing me this letter.

Thank you, Teresa.

Warmly,

Ruth Eimers

"Look, honey!" the young woman says, pointing to a footprint in the concrete. "I wonder if this is of the man who lived here."

Her husband leans down to inspect the mark. "How do you know it's a man?"

"Look how big it is!"

The man puts a hand to the woman's bulging belly. "Speaking of big . . ."

The woman smiles. "I know. Only three more weeks and she'll be here with us."

"I can't wait," the man says softly.

"*You* can't wait!" the woman says, laughing.

They stand together looking down at the footprint. "We can have that fixed," the man says.

"So you want to buy the house?" the woman asks.

The man nods. "You?"

"I do. I really like it. We can fix the bathroom and the kitchen for not too much and then it should last us for a long time."

The man reaches for his wife's hand. "Okay, let's go and tell the agent we want to make an offer." He starts to walk away, but his wife pulls on his hand.

She points to the footprint. "I want to keep this."

Her husband frowns. "*Why?*"

The woman looks out over the yard, into the lacy-leafed trees at the far back boundary, and shrugs. "I don't know," she says. "I just think it should stay here."

"We'll see," her husband says. "I don't want you tripping on anything."

The couple joins hands and walks around to the front of the house, where Sandy Bellman sits in a rocker on the porch, checking the messages on her phone.

"Ready?" she asks.

"Ready," they both say, smiling.

On a sunny October day, a mother and her four-year-old son are walking down the sidewalk. They pass a house with an elongated card table out front. There are many disparate objects piled onto it, and a sign saying *FREE!*

The woman touches a plate featuring bluebonnet flowers, a folded-up Christmas-themed apron, a small bowl full of stones. She picks up the bowl and her son says, "Can we have that?"

"What do you think it is?" the mother asks.

"It's *rocks,*" her son says.

"They aren't very pretty," the mother says, sifting through them.

"But they're special," the son says.

"What's special about them?"

The boy stares at the rocks. "I don't know, they just *are.*"

The mother hands the bowl to him. "Can you carry it?"

He nods solemnly.

"Be careful; if you drop it, it will break."

The mother picks up the apron and unfolds it. It's old, but it's in perfect condition. Kind of campy. She takes it and a pair of brass knuckles; her husband will get a kick out of them.

The rest of the items will stay on the table into the evening. After that, the man who bought the house will put them into a large trash bag that he will haul out to the curb for pickup in the morning.

When he comes inside, his wife will ask, "Did anyone want anything?"

"Not really," he will answer.

That night, in bed, with rain falling outside and her husband asleep beside her, the wife will finish reading the last few pages of a letter from the former owner that she was given by Teresa, the woman who lives down the block. Teresa won't be here much longer; she's getting married and moving into her fiancé's house, but she wanted whoever moved into Flo's house to have this.

When she finishes reading, the woman will look down at her husband and feel a rush of love nearly painful in its intensity. She will touch the top of his head gently, careful not to wake him, then slip out of bed to go into the baby's room. There, she will quietly slide open the top bureau drawer and place Flo's letter beneath tiny, folded t-shirts.

Early the next morning, birds will gather around water that has collected in a footprint in concrete. They will take turns bathing, and the droplets they shake off will capture light before they fall and disappear.

ACKNOWLEDGMENTS

There are so many people who should be acknowledged when you write a book. But this time, I want to acknowledge only two people. One is Beth Pearson, my copy editor, who understands everything about me as a writer. I have worked with her on many of my books, and it is always a joy. Always. Thank you, Beth, for your patience, expertise, sensitivity, and care.

The other person I would like to acknowledge is Kate Medina, my longtime editor. When she told me recently that she was retiring, I congratulated her. I knew it must have been a hard decision, and I admired the fact that she was leaving so much behind, even though what she was moving toward was as good or better. Still, I will miss her more than words can say. Literally.

What I can say is that I wanted to be a writer from the time I could hold a pencil. I remember being about four or five, lying on the floor of my bedroom, and practicing writing the capital letter E. I took creative license with the horizontal lines, so that my capital E looked less like a letter of the alphabet than a drawing of a comb. Never mind. The way I saw it, I was on my way. Very soon, I would be able to write, and then I could express on the page all that I felt inside.

As it happened, it took longer than I thought it would to

become a published writer. On the day I met Kate Medina, I was forty-four years old. "Where have you been?" she asked me. I had been doing a lot of other things, including working as a registered nurse for ten years, but now I had an esteemed editor (who sent me a bouquet of pink roses when she bought my first novel) telling me I should be writing more fiction. We were sitting in a beautiful restaurant in New York when she told me that, and I remember taking a very long time to respond—her words meant too much.

Kate and I went on to work on many more books together, and she always made me feel as though I were her only author. She took the time to respond—quickly—to any questions or comments I had. She offered good critiques, but she also had the generosity of spirit to call out things she just plain liked in a manuscript. Whenever I would see that she had written "Great!" in the margins of the hand-edited manuscripts she sent me, I would practically levitate in my chair.

For over thirty years, Kate listened to my ideas and my fears and my complaints. She sent me Godiva chocolates for Christmas. She hired the BEST assistants—self-assured, cheerful, intelligent, polite, and kind women. Most of all, though, Kate gave this oversensitive, insecure, yearning author a place to call home.

From the bottom of my heart, Kate.

ABOUT THE AUTHOR

Elizabeth Berg is the *New York Times* bestselling author of many novels, including *The Story of Arthur Truluv, Open House* (an Oprah's Book Club selection), *Talk Before Sleep,* and *The Year of Pleasures,* as well as the short story collection *The Day I Ate Whatever I Wanted. Durable Goods* and *Joy School* were selected as ALA Best Books of the Year. She adapted *The Pull of the Moon* into a play that enjoyed sold-out performances in Chicago and Indianapolis. Berg's work has been published in thirty-one countries, and three of her novels have been turned into television movies. She is the founder of Writing Matters, a quality reading series dedicated to serving author, audience, and community. She teaches one-day writing workshops and is a popular speaker at venues around the country. Some of her most popular Facebook postings have been collected in *Make Someone Happy, Still Happy,* and *Happy to be Here*. She posts regularly on her Substack column, "I've Been Thinking." She lives outside Chicago.

elizabeth-berg.net
Facebook.com/bergbooks

ABOUT THE TYPE

This book was set in Fairfield, the first typeface from the hand of the distinguished American artist and engraver Rudolph Ruzicka (1883–1978). Ruzicka was born in Bohemia (in the present-day Czech Republic) and came to America in 1894. He set up his own shop, devoted to wood engraving and printing, in New York in 1913 after a varied career working as a wood engraver, in photoengraving and banknote printing plants, and as an art director and freelance artist. He designed and illustrated many books, and was the creator of a considerable list of individual prints—wood engravings, line engravings on copper, and aquatints.